WILDERNESS:
THE OUTCAST

David
Thompson

LEISURE BOOKS NEW YORK CITY

Dedicated to Judy, Joshua and Shane.
And to Beatrice Bean, with the most loving regard.

A LEISURE BOOK®

June 2009

Published by

Dorchester Publishing Co., Inc.
200 Madison Avenue
New York, NY 10016

ISBN 10: 0-8439-6096-5
ISBN 13: 978-0-8439-6096-9
E-ISBN: 978-1-4285-0685-5

The name "Leisure Books" and the stylized "L" with design are trademarks of Dorchester Publishing Co., Inc.

Printed in the United States of America.

10 9 8 7 6 5 4 3 2 1

Visit us on the web at www.dorchesterpub.com.

A Vow of Vengeance

"Lou is still alive," Shakespeare said. "She's been taken by the Bloods."

A hot sensation spread from Zach's neck to the top of his head. "I'll count coup on all of them."

"Blue Water Woman only saw one, but there must be more." Shakespeare snagged Zach's sleeve as Zach turned. "Be careful. The Bloods are good fighters and damn clever. They'll be expecting someone to come after them. They'll be ready."

"They won't be ready for me," Zach vowed, and was out the door in long lopes.

P7-CHF-893

WILDERNESS #60:
THE OUTCAST

The End

He came out of the north, out of a land of virgin forests and icy winters, out of a land where lights danced in the night sky and the wendigo feasted on human flesh.

He had traveled so far, he could not say how many sleeps it had been. He was weary to his bones, but he didn't show it. He sat his horse straight and tall, his shoulders back, his chin high. No one would know to look at him that a dark secret hung over him like a cloud. No one would know that his own people had banished him.

He called himself the Outcast. That was all. It was not his name. He gave up his old name when he gave up his old life. Or, rather, when they made him give it up and cast him from the tribe.

The Outcast had been following a mountain stream for half a day when he became aware he was being stalked. There were three of them. They were young and clumsy. They intended to count coup on him. They intended to kill him and take his horse and his weapons and his parfleche. He almost felt sorry for them. Almost.

Others had tried to kill him. A lot of others. To many tribes, a stranger was an enemy to be slain on sight. A few tribes, too few, welcomed strangers in friendship. He had stayed with one of them until they found out what he had done and asked him to move on.

The sun was at its zenith. In the woods a jay screeched and a squirrel scampered high above from limb to limb. Small black and yellow birds played in a thicket.

The Outcast came to a clearing. He decided this was a good place for the stalkers to die. Climbing down, he patted his pinto. "Once again, old friend." He was fonder of the pinto than he had been of any horse he ever owned. He got it in trade from a Piegan who took it as a spoil on the field of battle. Few of his people owned pintos, and he had been the envy of many.

The Outcast led the pinto to the stream and let it drink. He stretched, saw his reflection, and frowned. He was big for his kind, big in frame but not in belly, and wore beaded buckskins typical of his people. His brow was high, his face long. He had black hair that reached his shoulders and was touched at the temples by early gray. A forelock hung over the middle of his brow. In his younger days the women had counted him handsome.

The women. At the thought, a tremble racked him, and he closed his eyes and groaned.

A nicker by the pinto reminded him he was about to have visitors. He slid his bow and quiver from the sheath *she* had made for him so very long ago. He slung the quiver over his shoulder and slid an arrow out and nocked it to the sinew string. Then he faced the forest.

"I am waiting. Come and slay me if you can." The Outcast doubted they understood him. The tongue of his people was different from most every other.

The challenge brought them into the open, as the Outcast knew it would. They had to accept it or bear the shame of cowardice, and no warrior worthy of the name could bear that taint. They wore buckskins of a style new to him, and their long hair hung in braids. One had a lance, the second a bow, the third a club with a metal spike, a weapon new to him, as well.

The one with the lance took a step forward and went on at length in his own tongue.

What he said, the Outcast had no idea. A challenge, no doubt. When the Outcast didn't reply, the young warrior leaned the lance against his chest and his hands flowed in sign talk. 'Question: You called?'

The Outcast stood as still as a tree.

'Question: Where you sit?'

The youth was asking where the Outcast was from, but the Outcast didn't answer.

'Question: You know sign talk?'

That was the first thing the Outcast would have asked. Of course he knew it. Most tribes did. He decided to try. They wouldn't listen but he would try. Setting down his bow and arrow, he signed, 'Go far. Go fast.'

The young warrior with the lance stiffened. 'This our land. We strong. You give horse. We let you live.'

So there it was. The Outcast picked up his bow and held it in front of him, and waited.

'Question: You want die?'

The Outcast drew the string back and sighted down the arrow. He let fly and the shaft flew true, the barbed tip entering the young warrior's right eye and bursting out the back of his head.

The second warrior drew back his own string and let his arrow fly.

Almost casually, the Outcast sidestepped. His hand a blur, he drew another arrow from his quiver and nocked it, and it was in the air heartbeats after the other's missed. His didn't. It caught the young warrior in the chest and spun him around.

That left the warrior with the club; he shrieked like an enraged mountain lion and bounded forward, the metal spike raised high. He was fast, but he wasn't faster than the arrow that penetrated his throat from front to back and left him on his knees, gagging and spitting blood.

The Outcast drew his tomahawk. The young warrior saw his shadow, glanced up, and tried to raise the strange club. The Outcast swung. His tomahawk bit deep, splitting the young warrior's forehead in half.

Wrenching the tomahawk loose, the Outcast stepped to the warrior he had shot through the chest. The man was thrashing and groaning. The fear of dying was bright in his eyes.

"You should have let your betters be," the Outcast said, and struck.

The scent of blood hadn't spooked the pinto as it would some horses. The Outcast slid his bow and quiver into his sheath and climbed back on. He stared at the bodies. Once, he would have scalped them, back when he was as young as they were and as foolish. He glanced at the sky. The vultures would come soon. They always did.

The Outcast went to ride on and caught himself. He was becoming careless. He dismounted, and pulled his arrows from the bodies. He also took the arrows from the quiver of the second warrior.

The strange club with the metal spike interested him. Bending, he hefted it. He was surprised at how light it was. It would be formidable at close quarters. It was too big for his parfleche, so he tied it on along with his bow.

On he rode.

The Outcast had been heading south for several moons now. Why, only the Great Mystery could say. He was deep in rugged mountains that reminded him of home. Mantled in thick timber, they were so high that some of the peaks were ivory with snow even though it was summer.

Presently the Outcast came to a valley with a large lake. From the heights he spied the wooden lodges of white men. His face hardened, and he placed his hand on his tomahawk.

He had found the lair of enemies.

Chapter One

If Zachary King lived to be a hundred years old, he would never understand women. No, he reflected. Make that a thousand. Their minds worked in strange ways. Female logic was no logic at all.

Take this latest instance. There was enough venison and elk meat in their larder to last weeks, but Louisa insisted he go and kill a grouse for supper. A grouse! When she knew he didn't like to pluck all those feathers. Lou loved grouse meat, though, and she was making a special meal, so she insisted he bring home a grouse and nothing else.

Women!

Zach stood on a slope a quarter of a mile above the lake at the center of King Valley and stared at his cabin on the north shore. Smoke curled from the chimney. Lou was baking a blackberry pie, one of his favorites. It mollified him, somewhat, for having to kill the grouse.

On the west shore stood his father's cabin, empty at the moment. His pa and his ma had gone off to St. Louis to have his pa's Hawken repaired.

On the south shore was the cabin of Shakespeare McNair and his Flathead wife, Blue Water Woman. Smoke rose from their chimney, too.

On the far east side of the lake stood the lodge of the Nansusequa, a friendly family of Indians from the East. They had gone off to the prairie to hunt buffalo. To Zach's considerable surprise, his sister, Evelyn, had gone with them. She hated to hunt. She hated to kill things. Yet off she went. She told Zach she was bored and needed something to do, which amused him considerably. The real reason she went was a young Nansusequa by the name of Degamawaku.

With everyone gone except Zach and Lou and Shakespeare and Blue Water Woman, the valley was quiet and peaceful. It was the middle of the summer and there wasn't much that needed doing. Zach could relax and take it easy for a change—if it weren't for his silly wife and her craving for a stupid grouse.

Women!

Zach sighed and resumed climbing. At that time of year and that time of day the grouse were in heavy woods where few meat eaters could get at them. He moved slowly, his thumb on the hammer of his Hawken. Around his waist were a brace of pistols, a Green River knife, and a tomahawk. Louisa liked to tease that he was a walking armory, to which he always retorted that he was still alive.

Zach wore buckskins and moccasins. With his long dark hair and the fact that his mother was a Shoshone, he knew that from a distance he appeared to be an Indian. His green eyes gave away his white inheritance.

Zach stalked as silently as a wolf toward a shelf

where the grouse liked to roost. He spied circles in the dust, which told him he was close; grouse liked to give themselves what his pa called "dust baths." This made no sense to Zach. How could it be a bath if it got them all dirty?

At a cluster of pines, Zach crouched. He scanned the vegetation, alert for movement. Grouse could move quickly when they needed to and take wing in a heartbeat. He was about to move on when a *whoop-whoop* came out of the undergrowth to his right—the cry of a blue grouse.

The largest were two feet high. Their feathers were usually a dusky blue, which accounted for their name. The females weren't as colorful as the males, who had bright orange over their eyes and orange and white on their chest. When courting, the males put on quite a display. They puffed up and fanned their tails and made a booming sound that could be heard a long way off. When he was a boy he'd asked his pa how they did that, and his pa had explained that grouse had pouches in their necks that filled with air and deflated to make the booms. Zach saw the pouches for himself the first time he carved up a grouse for a meal.

The *whoop-whoop* was repeated.

Zach placed each foot carefully, alert for dry twigs that might give him away.

A tree blocked his view. Zach peered around it and a tingle rippled down his spine.

There the grouse was, perched on a stump not twenty feet away. A male, but it wasn't puffed up. As he looked on, it tilted its head back and let out more whoops.

As slow as molasses, Zach raised the Hawken and wedged the hardwood stock to his shoulder.

Just as slowly, he thumbed back the hammer. He half feared the click would send the grouse into the air, but the bird went on whooping.

Zach gently squeezed the rear trigger to set the front trigger. He lightly placed his finger on the front trigger. All it would take was slight pressure. He fixed a bead on the grouse's head. The body was a bigger target, but the ball would make a mess of the meat. He held his breath and steadied the barrel, and when he was sure, he stroked the front trigger.

The Hawken belched smoke and lead, and the grouse suddenly had a neck with no head attached. The wings flapped a few times in reflex, and the body keeled over. A few kicks of its legs, then the blue grouse was still.

Zach smiled and walked toward the dead bird. Louisa would be pleased. He lifted the grouse by its feet; it was a plump one.

Blood dripped on one of his moccasins, and Zach's smile faded. Lou didn't like it when he came into the cabin with blood on his clothes. Setting the grouse down, he cut a whang from his sleeve and tied off the bird's neck so he wouldn't get any more on him.

Throwing the bird over his shoulder, Zach started down the mountain. He had gone a dozen strides when he drew up short. "I'm so eager to please her, I've turned foolish."

Zach put the grouse down. He uncapped his powder horn and commenced to reload his rifle. His pa had taught him early in life that it was the first thing a man did after taking a shot.

He was tamping the patch and ball down the barrel with the ramrod when he happened to glance at the mountains that ringed the lake to the north. For a split second he thought he saw a horse and rider, but when he blinked and raised a hand over his eyes to shield them from the sun, nothing was there. He figured it was a trick of the sun and the shadows.

Sliding the ramrod into its housing, Zach picked up the grouse and headed for the valley floor. He whistled as he walked.

Lou would be tickled pink.

Louisa King was worried. She knew how men were. She especially knew her man. Usually he was as wonderful a husband as any woman could hope for. But he was temperamental and prone to moods, and she hoped, she fervently hoped, he wasn't in one of his moods when he got home. She wanted everything to be perfect.

Lou didn't hold his moodiness against him. From what she'd been told, he had a rough childhood. It came from being a breed. Half white, half red, Zach was looked down on by both. A lot of whites regarded half-breeds as vicious and violent; a lot of red men believed that half-breeds weren't to be trusted because of the taint of white blood.

To Lou, it was just plain silly. People had no say over how they came into the world. They had no control over who their parents were. To be branded as inferior on account of an accident of birth was cruel. Besides, it wasn't the *blood* that counted; it was the *person*. It wasn't the *body* that mattered; it was the *personality* in the body.

In that regard—and Zach would be angry if she mentioned this to his face—her man had a kindly heart and a tender nature, even if he did hide it real well.

That was part of why Lou married him. The other part had to do with what Winona, Zach's Shoshone mother, called the Little Mystery.

The Great Mystery was the spirit in all things.

The Little Mystery was the special love that a woman and a man had for each other. The love that made a couple want to be together forever. It went beyond any other love. It reached into people's hearts, into the core of who they were. What was it about one woman out of all the women in the world that caused a man to want her more than any other? What was it about one man out of all the men in the world that instilled in a woman the sense that he was the man she wanted to be the father of her children?

At the thought, Lou stopped chopping carrots, placed a hand on her belly, and smiled. On an impulse, she put the knife on the counter and went into the bedroom. Attached to the back of the door was the full-length mirror she had pestered Zach into buying. He'd complained about the cost and the effort of bringing it all the way from Bent's Fort, but it was worth it.

Lou studied her reflection. She stared into her blue eyes, and then at her buckskins and again placed her hand on her belly. She appeared to be perfectly normal. No one could tell just by looking at her. She left the bedroom.

Taking the bucket off a peg, Lou went out. The bright sun, the birds singing in the trees, the beauty of the valley, stirred her. She hummed as she walked to the lake and dipped in the bucket.

Lou was so deep in thought that when a shadow

fell across her, she gave a start. Instantly, she reached for a pistol at her waist only to realize, to her horror, that she had left all her weapons in the cabin. Whirling, she exclaimed, "Phew! It's only you."

"That's a fine way to greet this old coon," Shakespeare McNair grumbled. He quoted his namesake, " 'My conscience hath a thousand several tongues, and every tongue brings in a several tale, and every tale condemns you for a villain.' "

Louisa laughed in delight and gave him a hug. McNair was one of her favorite people in the world. With his white hair and bushy white beard, he was old enough to be her great-grandfather. Yet he was as spry as Zach and as dear a man as ever drew breath. He wore buckskins, and his rifle was cradled in the crook of his left elbow. "What brings you over to our side of the lake?" she asked.

"I'm going hunting tomorrow and reckoned maybe that husband of yours would like to tag along." Shakespeare was telling only half the truth. His wife, Blue Water Woman, had told him to check in on Lou.

"Oh. He's off hunting right now, although he didn't want to. I sent him after a grouse for supper."

Shakespeare glanced at the bucket and then at her waist. "Have you no more brains than earwax, girl? Your man is off in the woods and you came outside unarmed? What were you thinking?"

Lou frowned. Zach was always on her, too, about not stepping out the door without a gun. He kept trying to impress on her that all it took was one mistake and she would pay with her life. As he put it to her once, "The wilderness has buried a lot of people and it will bury you, too, if you won't start taking it seriously. There's danger around every hill and behind every tree."

She'd laughed and told him that he exaggerated. But it became a sore point, so much so that she now said to McNair, "Please don't tell my husband. He'll have one of his fits, and I want everything to be perfect."

"You're about to tell him, I take it?"

Louisa blinked. "Tell him what?"

"Oh, come now." McNair grinned. "You're with child. It's as plain as your rosy cheeks and the glow you share with the sun."

Lou shouldn't have been surprised; McNair knew about her recent morning sickness. McNair and Nate King were best friends. McNair was so close to the family, in fact, that to this day Zach called him uncle. "Oh my. How many others know?"

"Just about everybody except your husband. There are none so blind as those who can't see past the nose on their face."

"That's not another quote from William Shakespeare, is it?"

"No, but it should be."

That was another thing Lou liked about McNair: his passion for the Bard. He had a big book of Shakespeare's plays and quoted them by the hour. How he could recite it all was beyond her. She was lucky if she remembered a few quotes from the Bible.

"So, am I right? Is this the night you drop fatherhood on his head and change his life forever?"

"You make it sound like a millstone."

"I'm only saying it's not to be taken lightly. It's

good you're both ready for it." Shakespeare paused. "You *are* both looking forward to having a baby, aren't you?"

"Well, it wasn't as if we planned it," Lou said, hedging. McNair had hit on the one thing that troubled her.

"Tell me, and be honest. Have the two of you talked this over? What it means to be a parent? The changes the baby will bring?"

"Not exactly, no."

"'Fair lady, do you think you have fools in hand?'" Shakespeare quoted. "You haven't said a word to each other, have you?"

"Of course we have," Lou said, a trifle indignantly. But the truth was, they'd talked about it only once, a short while back when she first thought she might be pregnant.

"Good. No one should jump in a poison ivy patch unless they like to itch a lot."

"You're comparing a baby to poison ivy? They have nothing in common."

"Tell that to a parent who has been up all night with a baby with the croup. Tell it to a parent who has to put up with all the caterwauling when a baby is teething. Tell it to a parent who has to change and wash diapers a thousand times. Tell it to a—"

Lou held up a hand. "Dear Lord. You make a baby sound like an affliction." She bent and lifted the bucket out of the water and Shakespeare immediately took it from her.

"I'll do the honors."

"Oh, please. I'm not helpless."

"Never said you were, girl. But a woman with a child in her brings out all the tenderness a man has. It's a good thing, too. It makes up for all the times men go around with blinders on."

"For a man, you sure don't think highly of your gender."

"Quite the contrary. I'm quite happy being male. The notion of being female scares me to death."

"Why?"

"I'd have to put up with men."

Lou laughed gaily. She headed for the cabin and gazed at the timbered slope beyond just as a jay took wing, squawking loudly. She idly wondered if something had spooked it, then put it from her mind. She had more important things to think about.

Up on the slope, the jay continued to squawk.

Chapter Two

The Outcast sat patiently on the pinto until the jay lost interest and flew away. Of all the birds, he liked jays least. Their shrill cries alerted everything within hearing. They were the bane of every hunter and warrior.

His brother used to argue that vultures were the worst birds because they ate rotting flesh and stank of death and were so ugly, but at least vultures were quiet.

The Outcast stared down the mountain. He could not tell much from that distance, but the white-haired man was plainly old and the sandy-haired woman, plainly young. He saw them talk and laugh and go into a wooden lodge.

A light jab of his heels sent the pinto down the slope. With a caution borne of experience, he rode slowly and hugged the shadows.

The Outcast was surprised to find whites so deep in the mountains, at least ten sleeps from the prairie, if not more. To his knowledge, no whites had ever penetrated this far.

He regarded white men much as he did jays. They were nuisances the world was better off without.

His first encounter with whites came when he was nineteen and went on a raid led by his uncle. Thirty warriors took part. They'd traveled south into the land of their longtime enemies the Nez Perce. But they were not fated to find a Nez Perce village. Instead they came upon a large party of bearded, hulking, coarse men with many horses and many beaver hides and many guns. The horses and the hides were incentive for his uncle to suggest they attack and kill the whites and take all they had, but the taking proved to be harder than any of them expected. They'd downed several of the whites with arrows and rushed in to slay the rest at close quarters. Only the whites drove them off, felling half a dozen warriors with their guns.

The Outcast had dragged his wounded uncle into the woods. There was a hole in his uncle's chest and a bigger hole in his back, and so much blood, it soaked the Outcast's leggings. His uncle had frothed at the mouth and was a while dying. The last words his uncle uttered was a plea to have his family looked after.

By then the whites had retreated to a cluster of boulders. The warriors tried to get at them, but the guns of the whites drove them back. Finally it was decided that too many had died, and they broke off the fight.

The Outcast learned important lessons that day. He learned that whites were not always easy to kill, and he learned to respect their guns.

Since then, the Outcast had fought whites on two other occasions. In one fight, the two sides had swapped arrows and lead, but nothing more came of it. In the other, the Outcast and six fellow warriors surprised four whites who were dipping pans in a stream and swirling the water around. It was most strange. But the whites had good horses and a lot of packs, and the Outcast had counted coup that day.

He never thought of whites as anything but enemies. They were like the Nez Perce, to be killed wherever he found them.

Now he came to a small clearing ringed by pines. Dismounting, he slid his bow and quiver from the sheath and glided lower. He must learn more about these whites. It wasn't wise to attack an enemy until you knew the enemy's strength. He wouldn't risk being seen until he was ready to be seen. He flattened himself on the ground about an arrow's flight from the wooden lodge.

The lodge, from what little the Outcast knew of the dwellings, was sturdily built. To one side was a pen for the horses. To the other were several small structures. In front of one of those were plump birds that clucked and pecked the ground. His mouth watered and his stomach growled as he imagined roasting the plumpest over a crackling fire.

Laughter came from within the lodge. The young woman must be goodnatured, he reasoned, to laugh so much. Everyone always told him whites were grim, but she wasn't.

From where he lay, the Outcast could see other dwellings across the lake. Smoke rose from only one. The wooden lodge at the west end and the long, low lodge to the east showed no signs of life. He wondered if they were empty, and if so, where the people who lived in them had gone.

Presently a rectangle of wood opened and out

came the old man and the young woman. The woman was smiling and happy. The old man placed a hand on her shoulder and said something in the white tongue that caused her to touch her belly and to shake her head. Then the old man kissed her on the forehead and went off around the lake. When he looked back, the woman waved, and he waved back.

The Outcast speculated that maybe the old man was her father.

Still holding her belly, the young woman walked to the water's edge and stood, staring across the lake. The wind fanned her hair, and she idly brushed at stray wisps.

She interested the Outcast, this woman. She was small and dainty, as the woman he never thought about had been, and she had a grace about her that he found appealing. The thought jarred him. He must remember who he was and what she was and not let her stir his feelings. He had given up the right to feel long ago.

Just then, to the west, someone yelled. The woman turned and smiled and ran to meet a young man who carried a dead grouse over his shoulder. They embraced with much passion, and the woman kissed him on the mouth. Together they moved toward the wooden lodge.

The Outcast dug his fingers dug into the earth until his knuckles were pale. Here was another reminder of the life he once had lived. He'd had a wife and a lodge, and been full of joy.

His eyes narrowed. There was something unusual about the young man. He'd taken him for a red man, but now that he was closer, the Outcast saw that her husband was a half-breed. Yet another surprise. He'd been told that whites didn't like breeds.

Not that it mattered.

Right then and there the Outcast made up his mind.

He was going to kill them.

Zach King couldn't believe the fuss his wife was making over supper. She insisted he wash up after he plucked and butchered the grouse, and made him don his best buckskins. She put a vase of those yellow flowers she liked on the table. She brought out her precious china and her fancy silverware. She even put a candle in the center of the table and lit it.

"Are we having company?" It was the only explanation Zach could think of. She never went to this much bother any other time. "Did you invite Shakespeare and Blue Water Woman?"

Louisa was spooning potato soup into a bowl. She had changed into her one and only dress, which she had sent for out of a catalog and picked up at Bent's Fort the last time they were there. "No. But he did stop by today and asked if you wanted to go hunting with him tomorrow."

"What is he going after? Did he say?"

Lou shook her head. "Why don't you have a seat, kind sir, and I'll bring the food over."

"I can help," Zach offered, although he really didn't want to. He considered cooking and the like woman's work. He offered only because if he didn't now and then, she carped that he never helped around the cabin.

"Not tonight. Tonight I'll wait on my lord and

master." Lou wanted him in fine spirits when she broke the news.

Zach pulled out the chair at the end of the table and sat. He was troubled. She never treated him like this unless she wanted something. Women were devious that way. They used their wiles to trick men into doing things the man wouldn't ordinarily do. He must be on his guard.

Bubbling with contentment, Lou brought over a steaming bowl of potato soup. She placed it in front of him and stepped back, smiling. "Here you go. Whites call this an appetizer. I know you like potato soup a lot. I added extra butter, too, just like you always want."

"Thank you." Zach picked up his spoon. He had taken several sips when he realized she was still standing there, watching him. "What's wrong?"

"I want to be sure you like it."

"I like it very much." Zach had learned early in their marriage never to say he disliked her cooking. Either it crushed her so that she sulked for days, or else it made her so mad, she went around slamming doors and giving him looks that would wither rock.

"Good." Lou beamed. Men were always in better frames of mind when they had full stomachs. She remembered her grandmother saying that the way to a man's heart was through his gut, and her grandmother had been right.

Zach swallowed more soup, and when she didn't move, he tactfully suggested, "Why don't you get a bowl and join me?"

"Oh. Sure. Sorry." Lou ladled only a little into her bowl. She wasn't all that hungry. The butterflies in her tummy were to blame. Taking the chair across from him, she took a tiny sip. "This is nice."

"I told you I liked it."

"No, not the soup. This." Lou motioned at the table and at them and at the room. "Our cabin. Our home. It's nice that we have four walls and a roof over our heads."

Zach deemed that a silly thing to say. Certainly it was nice. It beat sleeping in the rain and the snow.

"Who would have thought it would come to this."

"That we'd have a cabin? You told me you wanted one before we were married." Many times, Zach could have added but didn't.

"No, I didn't mean that. I meant us."

Zach was confused. They were man and wife. They lived together. That was the way of things. He decided not to say anything and devoted himself to his soup. No sooner did he swallow the last spoonful than Lou was at his elbow, taking the empty bowl.

"Now for the main course."

Zach marveled at how much time she must have spent cooking and baking. There was the roasted grouse. There were carrots and baked potatoes. There was gravy. There was freshly baked bread with butter. "It's not Christmas, is it?" he joked.

"I just wanted to show you how much I love you, how much you mean to me."

Zach's mental guard went up again. "I love you, too, Louisa. There was no need to go to all this bother."

"Love is never a bother. Love is love."

Zach fidgeted in his chair. There she went again

with another silly remark. *Of course* love was love. What else would it be? He ate in silence. When he finished the main course he was close to bursting. She brought over a thick slice of apple pie, and he sniffed it, savoring the scent. It was another of his favorites.

Lou sat back down and folded her hands in front of her. She waited until he forked a piece into his mouth, then cleared her throat. "How do you feel?"

"Like a snake that has swallowed a bird and is so swollen, it can't hardly move."

Lou didn't think much of his comparison, but she smiled and said, "Just so you're happy."

"I am."

"I want you to always be happy. I want *us* to always be happy. I want our children to be happy, too."

About to fork another piece into his mouth, Zach looked at her. He remembered how lately she had been sick in the morning. Suddenly the feast fit for a king took on a whole new meaning. "You're with child."

Lou smothered a frown. She'd wanted to break the news, not have it broken to her. "You don't have to say it quite like that. But yes, I am." She waited, and when all he did was bite the piece of pie off the fork, she goaded him with, "Well?"

"Well, what? You must take care of yourself. Don't lift heavy things. Don't eat a lot of sugar. Stuff like that."

Lou waited again, then said, "That's all you have to say?"

"What else? I'll need to make a cradle. Or maybe my pa will let us have the one they used for me and my sister. We'll tell them as soon as they get back. My ma can give you advice on all kinds of female stuff."

"That's all you can think of?"

Zach was uneasy. Her tone warned him that she was on the brink of anger, and he had no idea what he had done. "I'm right pleased. We've talked about having a baby and now we will."

"All you are is pleased? You're not giddy with excitement? You're not wonderfully happy?"

"Of course." Zach was none of that. But if saying he was kept her content, he would pretend.

"I mean, I go to all this trouble. I break the greatest news a wife can break to her husband, and you sit there and tell me you have to build a cradle."

"Do you want the baby to sleep on the floor?"

"Don't be ridiculous."

"All right. The bed, then?"

"Where the baby will sleep isn't the issue. The issue is how you reacted to the news."

"Be reasonable. It's not as if it was a huge surprise."

"A child is taking shape inside me as we speak. The miracle of new life. The greatest thrill we will ever know. And you sit there as if I just told you a weasel got one of the chickens."

"If a weasel got a chicken, I'd be mad. I'm not mad."

"You're not glad, either. Don't deny you're not. I can see it in your eyes."

Forgetting himself, Zach replied, "Don't tell me how I feel or how I don't feel. I should know better than you, and I tell you, I'm happy."

"Oh, Stalking Coyote."

Zach inwardly winced. She used his Shoshone name only when she was upset. She confirmed her distress by doing the one thing he couldn't stand for her to do.

Louisa burst into tears.

Chapter Three

Shakespeare McNair cleared his throat. "'To be or not to be, that is the question. Whether 'tis nobler in the mind to suffer the slings and arrows of outrageous fortune, or to take arms against a sea of trouble, and by opposing, end them.'"

Blue Water Woman looked up from her knitting. She was in the rocking chair, by the window. He was at the table honing his ax. If she had asked him once, she had asked him a thousand times not to hone his ax at the table. He always got tiny flakes all over. But did he listen? No. He was a man.

"Is there a point, or were you talking to hear yourself talk again?" Her English was excellent. She didn't speak it quite as well as Winona King, but she took great pride in how well she had mastered it. For a Flathead, the white tongue was as strange as a tongue could be.

Shakespeare harrumphed and stopped honing. "Did you just accuse me of being in love with the sound of my own voice?"

"What is it that whites say?" Blue Water Woman smiled sweetly. She wore a soft doeskin dress and moccasins. Her black hair, lightly streaked with gray, hung past her slender shoulders. "If the shoe fits . . ."

"A pox on thee, wench." Shakespeare bristled, and quoted the Bard, " 'I am well acquainted with your manner of wrenching the true cause the false way.' "

"There was a point to your *Hamlet*, then?"

"There is always a point to old William S.," Shakespeare informed her. "I was suggesting you might want to go over and talk to Lou tomorrow. She's breaking the news to Zach tonight, and I expect a storm cloud or three."

Blue Water Woman set the woolen cap she was making him in her lap. "That was your idea of suggesting I go see her? To be or not to be?"

"I thought it quite clever."

Letting out an exaggerated sigh, Blue Water Woman said, "I hear there are husbands who make sense when they talk. Husbands who use their own words and do not recite the words of a man who lived so long ago no one else remembers him."

Shakespeare slapped down the file. "Don't remember him?" he sputtered. "I'll have you know, woman, that he has been called the soul of his age. His writing is to words what flowers are to a mountain meadow."

"Perhaps it is best you recite him. Your own words make even less sense than his."

" 'Thou art so leaky, we must leave thee to thy sinking,' " Shakespeare countered.

"I am a boat now?"

Shakespeare smiled in anticipated triumph and declared, "If there is a purpose to women, I have yet to find it."

"Is that what you were doing with me last night in bed? Looking for my purpose?"

Shakespeare felt his face redden and burst out laughing. "Oh, that was marvelous. Your best yet. I swear, jousting with you is the most fun I know." He paused. "Next to what we were doing in bed, of course."

"You *are* male."

Coughing, Shakespeare changed the subject. "About Lou. She doesn't know Zachary like I do. They're apt to have an argument."

"I should think she knows her own husband." Just as Blue Water Woman knew hers and his fondness for butting into the affairs of others. To his credit, he always did it with the best of intentions.

"She's known him a few years. I've known Zach since he popped out of his mother and was swaddled in a blanket. I predict he won't take the news quite as merrily as Lou expects. So maybe you should go over and see if everything is all right. What with Nate and his other half gone, Lou has no one else to talk to."

"Wait a minute. Did you just say he *popped* out of Winona?"

"That might have been the term I used, yes."

"Babies do not *pop*. They are born. Giving birth can be hard on a woman. She goes through much pain, and if the birth does not go as it should, she can die."

"All right. *Popped* was a poor choice. Would *plunked* be better?"

"If I had a stick, I would beat you."

"Just so long as after you're done, you go and

visit Lou. I'm supposed to go hunting with Zach, and I'll sound him out about his feelings."

Blue Water Woman picked up her knitting, but didn't move the needles. "Do you ever regret that we have not had children?"

"If we had gotten together when we were Zach and Lou's age, then probably I would, yes." Shakespeare sighed. He had courted her back when they were that age. Her father, who didn't want any daughter of his taking up with a white man, forbade her to see him. Shakespeare had been crushed, but there was nothing he could do. They were forced apart, and later, both of them met and married someone else. Decades went by. Both their spouses died. They met again and discovered they still loved each other as passionately as ever. When he thought of all the years they could have had together but didn't, it was enough to moisten his eyes.

"Husband?"

Shakespeare realized she had been talking while he was adrift in their past. "Eh? What's that, my pretty?"

"I said we could adopt a child if you wanted."

"Land's sake. At our age?" Shakespeare chuckled, then shook his head. "As much as I might like to, this old coon's bones and joints aren't what they used to be. A two-year-old would waddle rings around me."

"I doubt that," Blue Water Woman said tenderly. "You can waddle quite fast when you put your mind to it."

"If that was a compliment, I'm a goat."

"Only when you are looking for my purpose.

And to set your mind at ease, tomorrow I will go see Louisa. I will pretend I am there to borrow sugar so she will not feel like I am prying."

"A marvelous idea. My pa used to say that the best way to deal with a problem is to nip it in the bud, before it becomes a problem."

"Wise advice."

Shakespeare nodded. "The only thing is, some problems you can't nip in the bud. You never see them coming."

Under the cloak of night the Outcast came down the slope and stood at the edge of the trees. He stared across an open space at the wooden lodge. He had never been this close to a white lodge before; it intrigued him. There had been no sign of a dog, so he felt safe crouching and crossing the open space, but he went slowly and with a hand on the hilt of his knife. He paused often to listen.

The horses in the corral were dozing. He stayed downwind to keep them from catching his scent. The small structure that housed the clucking birds was dark and quiet. He slipped past it and around to a square of glowing glass. Some sort of cloth had been hung over it on the inside, but there was a gap between the cloth.

His nerves tingling, the Outcast crept forward until he could reach out and touch the lodge if he wanted. It was made of hewn logs, one on top of the other, the niches caulked with what appeared to be clay. He inched higher, until his eye was at a corner of the glass, and peered inside.

The breed and the young woman were sitting on a strange wooden seat next to a large piece of wood on four wooden legs. The breed appeared to be upset. The young woman was weeping.

It shocked the Outcast so much, he ducked back down. The last time he saw a woman cry had been the terrible day that changed his life. The day that got him banished from his tribe. He wondered what the breed had done to make her shed tears. Then he remembered that sometimes women did not need a reason. They just cried to cry.

The Outcast cautiously took another peek. The breed was talking in low tones. The young woman had her head bowed. She answered him, but so softly, the Outcast barely heard her words.

For some reason the Outcast could not take his eyes off them. He had not been this near to people, except for the three warriors who tried to kill him, in many moons. He had not been this near to a woman . . . he did not like to think how long that had been. He stared at her, at her sand-colored hair and slight frame and the tears trickling down her cheeks, and he felt a strange stirring. His throat constricted, and he almost made the mistake of coughing to clear it.

The Outcast did not understand what was happening to him.

The young woman looked up, and seldom had the Outcast seen such sadness. She was in the throes of torment. He wished he knew the white tongue. Maybe then he could make some sense of what she was saying. Whatever it was, it upset the breed even more. The breed suddenly stood and leaned on the table and said something almost savagely, then turned and moved away from the window.

Too late, the Outcast heard the scrape of wood. The half-breed was coming out. Quickly, the Outcast retreated to the opposite corner and crouched. He drew his knife. He was ready to kill the breed if the man came close. He considered whether to stalk him and kill him anyway.

Then a horse nickered and stamped.

The Outcast had forgotten about the horses. His back was to the corral, and whirling, he saw that a sorrel had its head high and its ears pricked and was looking right at him. He had been careless. He figured the breed would investigate. Staying low, he ran toward the trees, but he went only a short way and dived flat. Hidden in the veil of darkness, he waited. But the breed still did not appear.

Puzzled, the Outcast crawled in a wide loop. Finally he spotted a silhouette at the water's edge. The breed was pacing back and forth, his hands clasped behind his back. The Outcast was surprised to hear him muttering to himself. Men should not mutter. Women, yes, but not warriors. He reminded himself that whites were not warriors and this breed was half white.

The breed was so engrossed, it would be easy to crawl close and slay him. The Outcast was tempted. Then the rectangle of wood opened again and out came the young woman. She crossed to the breed and quietly addressed him.

The Outcast wanted to see their expressions. He could tell more if he could see their faces. He had to gauge their feelings by the way they said their words. The young woman said them sadly. The breed responded angrily. Suddenly the young woman cried out, threw her arms wide, and embraced him, sobbing. He embraced her, and for a long while they stood still and were silent save for the young woman's sniffling.

Again the Outcast felt that strange constriction in his throat. It troubled him. He watched, and wondered why he did not rise up and rush them. He would be on them before they realized he was there. Two strokes of his blade and the deeds would be done. But he didn't rise. He stayed flat on the ground.

The pair moved slowly toward their lodge. They exchanged a few soft words. The breed dabbed at the young woman's face with his sleeve, and she laughed.

The Outcast remembered how another woman, in another time, once laughed as merrily, and his insides churned. *I am a worm*, the Outcast thought, and closed his eyes. He must not think about her. He must not think about her. He must never, ever think about her. The image faded, and the Outcast was relieved. It bothered him, this new weakness. The young white woman was to blame. Something about her was affecting him. But why that should be mystified him.

The rasp of the wood flap closing brought the Outcast out of himself. The pair were back inside.

The Outcast frowned and made for the woods. When he came to the pinto, he climbed on and rode around the west end of the lake, past a dark, quiet lodge.

The south shore was bordered by the grassy valley. There was no cover except the grass, but that was enough for the Outcast. He left the pinto in the trees and crawled toward the other lodge with glowing glass. Once again he reached the lodge without being detected. Once again he put his eye to a corner of the glass. Inside was the old white man with hair the color of snow, and one other. That it was a woman did not surprise him; that she was an Indian, did.

At first the Outcast took her for a Nez Perce, but as he studied her features and her hair and her dress, he changed his mind. She was a Flathead. His tribe had had few dealings with them, and those they had were always at the point of a lance or a knife. He guessed that she had seen at least fifty winters, but he never had been good at judging the age of women. This one was uncommonly attractive and possessed a grace and dignity that impressed him.

The Outcast wondered if the white man had bought her. That happened sometimes among other tribes. The Crows, he had heard, made a habit of it. But then the Crows had their minds in a whirl. It was said that women ruled their tribe, which had made the men of his own tribe laugh. It was also claimed that Crow men used the women in common and that the Crows took their women by stealing them, which made no sense. Why steal a woman if you were going to let other men have her? Maybe it wasn't true. Rumors about other tribes were not always based on fact.

The white hair moved out of sight of the window, and the Outcast tensed, thinking he was coming outside. But no, the man reappeared holding something the Outcast had never seen before. He did not know what to make of it. It was square, and consisted of many white sheets with blacks marks on them. The white man opened it and then began talking in a loud voice, with much gesturing.

The woman rolled her eyes. She sat in a marvelous thing that rocked back and forth. She was using long metal needles to weave a garment. She said something that caused the old man's cheeks to grow red.

Then both of them grinned.

The Outcast realized they were very much in love, these two. He remembered the time he had been in love, and was mad at himself.

He had seen enough.

The Outcast ducked down and left. Apparently there were only the two men and the two women in the entire valley. Whoever lived in the other lodges must be gone, or the lodges would be aglow with light.

The Outcast had gone a short way toward the trees when there was a tremendous splash in the lake. He looked, imagining it was a fish, but whatever it was had gone back under, leaving ripples.

Once on the pinto, the Outcast reined to the west. He would spend the night deep in the timber. He must get plenty of sleep. Although he had been banished from his tribe, he had not stopped being a warrior. He still counted coup.

And he had new enemies to slay.

Chapter Four

They came out of the heart of the darkness. There were seven of them—short, stocky warriors as different from other mountain and plains tribes as the night from the day.

Their buckskins were crude and lacked whangs. The sleeves flared from the elbows to the wrists, and on the right hip of each legging were three concentric circles painted in black. They carried ash bows and had quivers filled with arrows fletched with raven feathers. The hilts of their knives were carved from antlers, and the blades were iron.

Most remarkable of all were their faces: low foreheads, thick eyebrows, eyes like black pitch, jutting jaws, and scars. Scars in intricate patterns that covered every inch of skin on their face, deep scars that formed symbols. What they stood for, only the short men could say.

The men moved at night and laid up during the day. Less chance of being seen that way.

They were a secretive people. Bitter experience taught them the need for it. Once they lived far to the south along a great bay. Life had been good. They hunted and fished and ate the hearts of their enemies, as their forefathers had done for more winters than there were blades of grass.

Then a new tribe came. A large tribe in the thousands, compared to their paltry hundreds. The warriors rode on fleet, giant dogs, which the Tun-kua later learned were called horses, and did not like having their hearts eaten. They made fierce war on the Tun-kua, or Heart Eaters, as they called themselves, and it became apparent that unless the Heart Eaters fled, they would be wiped out.

Councils were held. They could not go south. There was nothing but water. They had canoes, but only a few, and they always stayed close to shore. They were not a seafaring people.

They could not go east. That way lay vast swamps and bayous infested with alligators and snakes.

The west did not appeal to them. The land was dry and hot, much of it desert, and claimed by a tribe they held in great dread, the Shis-Inday.

The only way, then, was for the Heart Eaters to go north. They packed their possessions on travois drawn by dogs, and in the dead of night left the land they loved, bound for the unknown. They crossed a near-endless prairie of waving grass. The plain did not suit them, so they turned to the northwest, and after countless sleeps came to towering mountains capped by snow.

The Heart Eaters marveled. They had never seen mountains so high. They explored and were amazed to discover that while a few tribes had laid claim to territory here and there, much of the mountains belonged to no one. They penetrated deep into the interior, deeper than anyone had ever gone, so deep that the valley they chose had never been trod by human feet. It became their new home. Here they would be safe.

Or so they thought.

Now, hiking briskly up a boulder-strewn slope, the lead warrior paused and looked back the way they had come. He could not see their valley or their village, but he looked anyway.

"You keep doing that," remarked Splashes Blood, the warrior behind him. "What is it you look for, Skin Shredder?'

Skin Shredder was thinking of one of his wives and their new child, but he did not say that. "By the rising of the sun we will reach the pass."

Splashes Blood grunted. "They say we cannot get through. They say the Bear People blocked the pass with rocks and dirt."

"There will be another way."

"I hope so. We both lost brothers. I lost Ghost Walker and you lost Stands on Moon."

"The Bear People must be punished," Skin Shredder declared. "Our brothers will look down from Mic-lan and be pleased with us for avenging them." In their tongue, Mic-lan was Sky Land, where warriors went after they died. A place of beauty and plenty, with enough hearts to eat for all. "They will honor us with a feast when we join them."

Splashes Blood had more on his mind. "It is said the Bear People have horses. It is said their women are almost as big as they are. It is said they have strange sticks that make a noise like thunder and can kill from far away. It is said they are—"

"Who says all this?" Skin Shredder cut him off.

"Spirit Walker spied on them before the pass was blocked. He saw many wonders."

"Are you a child, to be impressed by dogs and size? We are Tun-kua. We are the Heart Eaters. We will capture these Bear People and take them back to our village so that all may take part in eating their hearts. Their medicine will be ours." That was the part Skin Shredder looked forward to the most, the eating and the power that would come from it.

"I would like to have one of their women."

"Have as in eat or have as in the other?"

"The other." Splashes Blood quickly added, "Before you say anything, yes, I know Tun-kua are only to share their blankets with other Tun-kua. But I have long wondered what it would be like to have a Bear Woman."

"The Bear People are huge and ugly and smell. Were you to lie with one of their females, she would crush you between her legs."

"I had not thought of that," Splashes Blood admitted. "They do have big legs. My women have strong legs and theirs are not half as big."

Skin Shredder scanned the ridge above for the silhouette of a cliff. This talk of mating with a Bear Woman bothered him. It would be the same as mating with an animal. He reminded himself that his friend had always been woman hungry. Of all the Tun-kua, only Splashes Blood had four wives. Skin Shredder had three, and there were times of the month when that was two too many.

"It is good to hunt hearts again," Splashes Blood said.

On this Skin Shredder agreed. In the old days

there had been many hearts to eat. But now they lived so deep in the mountains, with so few tribes anywhere near, the eating of hearts was rare. Human hearts, anyway. Just thinking of eating one again made his mouth water.

"Don't do that."

"I can't help it," Louisa said and sniffled. "It is what people do when they are upset."

"Not all people." Zach could count the number of times he had cried on one hand and have fingers left over. His father and mother hardly ever cried, either. He could remember his father crying only twice: once when his mother lay at the verge of death, and again when his sister was kidnapped by a white woman in revenge for his pa's shooting her brother.

Lou sniffled again. Here she had tried so hard to make this meal special so that when she broke the good news he would be happy, and instead he was acting as if he didn't really want a baby.

"I will leave if you don't stop."

"Please," Lou said softly.

"Please what?"

"Don't be this way. It means so much to me and I want it to mean as much to you."

"It does."

"Then why aren't you smiling and jumping up and down and acting all giddy as most men would?"

"When have I ever acted giddy over anything?"

Lou raised her head and looked at him, tears trickling down her cheeks. "We're talking about our first baby."

"And I'm saying you can't judge me by what

other men do. Just as I would never expect you to act like other women. We are each of us different. We do as we are, not as others are."

"You're changing the subject. Why aren't you happy over the baby?"

"Oh, hell." Zach got up and went to the door. As he worked the latch, he said, "I need some air."

"Don't go."

Zach had to. He was mad. He was afraid he might say something he would regret and upset her more, and he would spare her that. So he went out and walked down to the lake. He hardly noticed the night sky or the wind or the water lapping the shore. He began to pace. His head was in a whirl, as the Shoshone would say. He wished his parents were home. Often when he was troubled, a talk with them soothed him.

He loved Lou dearly, but women could be a trial. She expected him to act like a simpleton when they faced the most serious event of their life. She didn't look past the baby part to what came next. But he did, and it worried him. He considered what he should say to make her understand, then realized he was muttering to himself.

The door opened.

Louisa's heart had torn in half when he walked out on her. She started to cry in earnest but stopped herself. She mustn't break down. She must find out what was bothering him. It did no good to weep over something she didn't understand.

Dabbing at her nose with her sleeve, Lou walked to the lake. She quietly stared at him, and he stared at her, and neither of them said anything until he gruffly demanded, "Well?"

"I thought we should talk some more."

"It would help if you would listen. Your tongue works better than your ears."

At that, Lou flinched. He rarely cast barbs at her. "All right. I'm listening with all that I am. What do you have to say for yourself?"

Zach struggled for the right way to express his feelings. "We're going to have a child."

"And you don't want one. I get that now."

"Damn it."

Lou flinched again. He hardly ever cursed. Some men did all the time, but not him or his pa. "What?"

"That is the one thing you do that drives me madder than anything."

"What?" Lou repeated, confused.

"You put words in my head. I hate that. You jump to conclusions and you put words in my head that were never there. I never said I didn't want a baby. I never even *thought* it."

Lou composed herself. He had a point. She had jumped to this conclusion, and that must be what was troubling him. "I'll try not to do that. But can you tell me what is the matter so I can understand? That's all I really want, is to understand."

"We are going to have a child and I don't know if I'm ready."

Lou was still confused. "Ready how?"

Zach hesitated. It was so hard to admit it. He had to clear his throat to say, "I don't know if I'll make as good a father as you will a mother."

"That's ridiculous. You'll make a fine father. Why would—"

"I thought you just said you would try harder?" Zach interrupted.

Lou dabbed at her nose again. "Yes, I did. I'm sorry. Go on. Why don't you think you'll be any good at it?"

"Because I'm me."

"I'm sorry, but that makes no sense. Of course you're you. Who else would you be?"

Zach gazed out over the lake. "Until I met you, I was what some would call reckless. I have a temper, and time and again it got me into trouble. Time and again I spilled blood. The irony, as my pa would call it, didn't escape me."

"The irony?"

"I always hated being called a breed. People look down their noses at breeds. They think breeds are violent and vicious, and I despised them for that. But then one day it hit me. I had become the very thing I despised them for thinking I was. If that isn't ironic, I don't know what is."

"What does that have to do with our baby?"

"It got so bad, I have a reputation for being a killer. I was arrested by the army and put on trial, remember? It's a wonder I'm standing here now, talking to you. I might have been hanged."

"I was there. I know all about your past. You've kept no secrets from me," Lou said. "But that was then. This is now. You've changed, Zach. You're not the same person you once were."

"People never change. They act in new ways, but the old part of them is still buried deep inside." Zach sighed. "I act mature now, yes, but I still have a temper. I just control it better."

"Then you have changed, and for the better."

"Will you please listen?" Zach was growing exasperated. He took several deep breaths to calm himself, then went on. "People *never* change. They just act in different ways. So when we have our baby, I'll be as fine a father as I can be. But will that be enough?"

"Why wouldn't it?" Lou was struggling to grasp what he was getting at, and worried she was upsetting him even more.

"Because I'll still be me. I'll still be the man who doesn't abide insults. I'll still be the man who wants to smash the face of anyone who looks down their nose at him. I'll still be the same Zach King who got into trouble all those times and was nearly hanged."

Comprehension dawned, and Lou almost laughed. "Oh, you glorious fool, you."

"Excuse me? Did you just call me a fool?"

"You were arrested for killing a man who was selling guns to the Indians and trying to stir up a war, and you were acquitted. So let's not hear any more about that. As for your temper, you hardly ever lose it anymore, so you can change, no matter what you think. No, what's bothering you is that our child will be a half-breed, and you don't want it to go through the hell you did."

"There's that, too."

"But don't you see? No child of ours will suffer as you did because we won't let it. I know you. You'll protect our son or daughter as fiercely as a mother bear protects her cubs."

Zach managed a wry grin. "So now I'm a fool and a female?"

"But you do want this baby, don't you?"

"More than anything in the world."

Louisa flooded with emotion. "I love you, Zach King."

"And I love you, broken ears."

She flew into his arms, and for a long while they just stood there, saying nothing because there was no need.

Chapter Five

Shakespeare McNair whistled as he rode. The sun was shining in a bright blue sky, birds were singing in the trees, and the lake was a picturesque playground for mallards, geese, mergansers, and other water fowl. All was right with the world, and he liked his world that way.

Shakespeare rode slowly. His white mare, like he, was getting on in years. He had thought about getting another horse and letting her while away her days in the corral, but she was like him in another regard—she liked to get out and around, and became downright ornery if she was cooped up too long. In that respect, she also reminded him of a certain Flathead lady he knew. He chuckled at the thought.

Shakespeare passed Nate and Winona's cabin and rose in the stirrups to stare intently at the dwelling of their elder offspring and daughter-in-law. All appeared tranquil. Smoke curled from the chimney. The chickens were pecking. He gathered that everything was all right. He hoped so. He dearly adored both Zach and Lou, and regarded them as family. The boy had been calling him uncle since he could toddle.

Shakespeare drew rein a dozen feet out. "Hail the cabin!" he hollered. "Are you decent in there?"

The door opened, framing Lou. She had on a dress and an apron, and her hands were on her hips. "What else would we be at this time of day? That is not all women think about, unlike some men I could mention."

"Now, now," Shakespeare said. "He can't help it. At his age, most males are randy as goats."

"I was talking about you."

"Me?" Shakespeare declared in mock indignation. "Why, I'm scandalized. I'll have you know, young lady, that at my age women are not the be-all and end-all. Waking up in the morning is."

"That's not what Blue Water Woman told me."

"How's that?"

"We were at Winona's not long ago and your darling wife happened to mention that she can't hardly get her housework done for you pawing her all the time."

Shakespeare's indignation was no longer mock. "She said that? The wench! Her kisses are Judas's own children. There's no more faith in her than in a stewed prune."

Laughing, Lou came outside. She squinted against the glare of the sun and ran her hands down her apron. "A man your age, I should think you would be flattered."

"A man my—!" Shakespeare put a hand to his chest as if stricken. "What have I done, child, that you prick me so? Am I remiss in my bathing? 'Love talks with better knowledge, and knowledge with dearer love,'" he quoted.

"Now, now. Don't get all pouty. Your wife loves you as dearly as she loves anything and would never say something that would hurt your feelings."

"Too late for that," Shakespeare huffed. " 'You cannot make gross sins look clear.' " He lowered his hand. "But we'll drop it for now. I'll take this up with her when I get back."

"Don't you dare. She'll ask how you found out."

"I'll lie."

"She's too smart for that. Sometimes I think she's the smartest person in our valley. She'll figure out that since only Winona and I knew, and Winona is gone, it had to be me."

"And what of me, child?" Shakespeare asked. "Have I no brain? Aren't I as intelligent as my wife?"

"Oh, I am sure you are," Lou hastily assured him. "But smart is not the same thing as intelligent."

"Since when? That's like saying a scrambled egg isn't the same thing as an egg cooked with the yolk staring at you. They are both eggs."

To Lou the distinction was obvious. "Intelligent is when you have a really good brain. Smart is when you know how to use it."

"Dear Lord. Now I'm twice stricken." Shakespeare drew his knife and held it out to her, hilt first. "Here. Stab true and put an end to my misery."

"Oh, please. You're smart, too. Now quit acting silly and climb down. I'm baking a cake."

"Celebrating something, are we?" Shakespeare asked, and grinned and winked. "Did it go as well as you seem to suggest?"

Lou happily nodded. "It went fine." She placed

her hand flat on her apron and looked down at herself. "He's made his peace with the idea of being a father."

"I knew he would. I have confidence in that boy." Shakespeare launched into another quote. "'The youngest son of Priam, a true knight, not yet mature, yet matchless. Firm of word, speaking in deeds and deedless in his tongue.'"

From inside the cabin came a chuckle. "Lordy. If I have to put up with that all day, I might as well stay home." Zach strolled out, his Hawken cradled in the crook of an elbow. "My wife tells me you want to go hunting."

"That I do, Horatio Junior," Shakespeare confirmed. "A black bear has been sniffing around our cabins of late, and unfortunately for him or her, as the case might be, my wife would like a new bearskin rug."

"I've been seeing bear sign, too," Zach said. "Come to think of it, the bear might have been around last night. I heard one of the horses act up, but didn't go for a look-see."

"Getting lazy in your young age, are we?"

"I had something on my mind at the time." Zach didn't elaborate. Instead, he took Lou's hand in his and asked, "Are you sure it's all right? We might be gone most of the day."

Lou beamed and kissed him on the cheek. "Go on. Have fun. I have the cake to bake and a list to compose of all the things we'll need to get before the baby comes."

"Uh-oh," Shakespeare said. "It's begun. Brace yourself, son. Once a wife starts making a list of jobs for her man to do, the poor cuss never has any time to himself."

"Goodness, how you exaggerate," Lou retorted. "To listen to you talk, a person would think all women were shameless gossips and cruel task-masters."

"'You speak an infinite deal of nothing,'" Shakespeare quoted. "And you put words in my mouth, besides."

Zach almost commented that she was good at that. But after last night, he decided he better not. "Take care while I'm gone. Don't lift anything heavy."

"Land's sake," Lou said. "I'm not that far along yet. Don't treat me as if I'm fragile when I'm not."

"Whatever you do," Zach cautioned, "don't step outside without a weapon."

Lou glanced at McNair, wondering if he would tell Zach she had done just that the day before. But all Shakespeare did was smile. "Don't worry about me. I'll be perfectly fine," she said.

Flat on his belly behind a log, the Outcast watched the half-breed and the old white ride off. That they were together suited his purpose.

The Outcast had lain awake long into the night, thinking. He had a plan. The first part of that plan involved the young white woman.

He stayed where he was until the breed and the old man were lost to view to the south. Then he rose, and with his bow in hand, crept along the tree line until he was on the side of the lodge opposite the square of glass. Swiftly, he crossed the open space and pressed his back to the logs.

He edged toward the front. Peering around the corner, he saw that the young woman had left the rectangle of wood open. From within came humming. She sounded very happy. For a few moments that gave him pause, but only a few. He crept around the corner.

Inside the cabin, Louisa was mixing cake ingredients. She added half a cup of sugar. One of her weaknesses was her sweet tooth. Zach often teased her about it, but she had loved sweets since she was a little girl, and whenever they went to Bent's Fort she made sure they brought sugar home.

Outside the cabin, the Outcast leaned his bow against the logs and drew his knife. He peeked inside. Wood covered the ground. Part of one side was made of stone. There was a square of wood with four long legs, like the old man and the Flathead had in their lodge, and those things they sat on. It was so unlike the lodges of his people. Whites were strange.

Inside the cabin, Lou went to a cupboard and took down the bowl of eggs she had gathered that morning from the chicken coop. She wished she had milk. Water would do, but milk was better. She kept suggesting to Zach that it would be nice if they had a cow, but her suggestion seemed to go in his ears and bounce back out. She was beginning to think that being subtle with a man didn't work. The only way for a woman to get her man to listen was to walk up and whack him on the head. She giggled.

Outside the cabin, the Outcast wondered what she found so amusing. He slid one foot inside and then the other. He held the knife low, the blade out. A single thrust and he could kill her.

Lou set down the spoon. She could use a few more eggs. She started to turn, thinking she would go out to the coop and see if the chickens had laid more. Her hands drifted to her apron, to her belly, and she looked down at herself. She thought of the new life inside of her and marveled at the miracle. She was both overjoyed and scared. Scared that something might go wrong. Both Winona and Blue Water Woman had said they would be there for her, and that helped.

Shock gripped the Outcast. The glow on the young woman's face, her gesture in placing her hands over her stomach. He had seen the one he never thought about do that many times when the spark of new life was kindled in her. *The white woman is pregnant.* It jolted him. It shouldn't have, but it did.

Lou closed her eyes and gently rubbed small circles across her belly. "What should we call you?" she wondered out loud. Which was silly since they had no idea whether it was a boy or a girl. Zach kept saying it would be a boy and was already talking about the hunts they would go on and how he would teach the boy to track and fish and hone knives and how to read the stars at night.

The Outcast almost trembled. This young white woman reminded him so much of *her*. Part of him wanted to slay her then and there, to plunge his knife into her body again and again and again. Another part of him—the part that had cried with happiness the day *she* told him the good news, the part he thought he had wiped from his being—stirred deep within him.

"If you're a girl we can call you Judith or Kathleen or maybe Karen. I've always liked those names. Or how about Beatrice? Would you like to be called Bea?"

The Outcast fought down his shock. He must remember she was white, and his enemy.

"If you're a boy, we could call you Nate, after Zach's pa, or Shakespeare, after the nicest man who ever lived. Your pa-to-be has his mind set on a name, but he won't tell me what it is. He says it's a secret and he'll only say after he's holding you in his arms."

The white woman's voice, so low and soft, reminded the Outcast of *her* voice. He edged forward.

"I don't know why he's keeping it a secret. But then, he's a man, and men do the silliest things. But I wouldn't trade mine for all the silk and jade in China." Lou giggled, and rubbed her stomach some more. "Listen to me, talking to you as if you can hear me. I guess Zach isn't the only silly goose in this family."

The Outcast moved closer. He was almost within striking range.

"If you are a girl, I want you to know I'll be the best mother I can possibly be. I may not always do everything right, but I'll always try."

The Outcast's insides were twisted into a knot. He wished she would stop rubbing. The memories were almost more than he could bear.

"One last thing and I'll stop babbling. This is a hard life, baby. We like it to be nice and often it is. But hard times come whether we like them or not. I lost my ma much too early. I lost my pa to hostiles. I pray to God I get to live longer than they did. I pray I see you grow to be a woman, and see you with a husband of your own one day. I pray I can hold my grandchildren in my lap and rock them in front of the fireplace in the evening. That would make me happier than anything I can think of."

The words were meaningless to the Outcast. Her expression, though, said more than words ever could. He stopped and looked down at his knife, and when he looked back up, the woman was staring at him in bewilderment.

Lou couldn't believe her eyes. Her heart pounded in her chest. She realized she had left the front door open. If Zach had warned her about that once, he had warned her a hundred times. Worse, her pistols were on the dresser in their bedroom and her rifle was propped against the wall over by the front door.

The Outcast willed his arm to move. He willed his hand to bury the knife. He did not need her alive. She would serve his purpose as well dead.

Fear washed over Lou, but she did not let on that she was afraid. Zach told her once that she must never show fear to an enemy.

The Outcast's hand didn't move. Nor did he. He saw that she was unafraid, and his respect for her climbed. Then he remembered why he was there. Taking two long steps, he touched the tip of his blade to her throat.

Lou swallowed, but that was all. She looked into the warrior's dark eyes, and she forced a smile. "How do you do? My name is Louisa King. Who might you be?"

The Outcast cocked his head and studied her. This wasn't what he expected. This wasn't what he expected at all.

Lou was trying to tell which tribe he was from. She thought at first he might be a Ute since the Ute lived closest to King Valley, but she had seen

Utes and they were different. He wasn't a Crow or a Nez Perce or any of the other Indians she was familiar with. The tribe he most reminded her of were the Blackfeet, but his face and his buckskins were not quite as theirs were.

The Outcast was confused. Here he was, holding a knife to her neck, and all she did was stare at him. Most enemies would fight or cringe in fright.

Lou knew a little Shoshone, so she tried that. She didn't realize she still had her hands on her belly until she saw him look down at them.

The Outcast was thinking of *her* again. Of how happy he had been when the baby was born. He remembered its wail when the lance pierced its body, and he broke out in a cold sweat.

Lou wondered why the warrior was just standing there. She'd thought she was a goner, but now she wasn't so sure. Maybe he wanted her alive. She kept on smiling and said quietly, "I will be your friend if you will let me. Me and my husband both." Those last words weren't entirely true. Were Zach to walk in the door, he'd kill the warrior before he could blink.

The Outcast shook himself and stepped back. He had come in determined to slay her, and now he couldn't. He didn't understand what he was feeling. Or did he, and he was unwilling to admit it? The Outcast started to raise his free hand to his brow and caught himself. He must be strong. He must not let her stir his memories. It would be so easy to kill her. She was so small, so fragile. Then he saw her eyes and was startled. He had not noticed until now that they were blue. Blue had been *her* favorite color. The baby was bundled in a blue blanket on that terrible day, and in his mind, as vivid as if it were happening again, he saw the splash of red against the blue, and a growl of torment escaped him.

Lunging, the Outcast gripped the white woman by the throat.

Chapter Six

Shakespeare McNair waited until they were half a mile south of the lake. Then he coughed and casually asked, "So, is there any news you care to tell me, Horatio Junior?"

Zach was scouring the ground for sign. "None that I can think of. And how many times have I told you not to call me that?"

"None at all?"

"I expect my parents back in a week or two. And there were elk at the lake this morning." Zach scratched his chin and pretended to ponder. "Oh, wait. Lou and I saw two squirrels the other day. She thought they were downright adorable."

"Which is more than I can say about her husband."

Zach shifted in the saddle. "Pardon me?" he innocently asked.

"'You are a knave, a rascal, an eater of broken meats,'" Shakespeare quoted. "'A base, proud, shallow, beggarly, three-suited, hundred-pound, filthy worsted-stocking knave.'"

"Why, Uncle Shakespeare, whatever do you mean?"

Shakespeare wasn't done. "'Thou cruel, ingrateful, savage and inhuman creature.' To think I bobbed you on my knee and tickled you and let you pull on my whiskers, and this is how you treat me?"

"You're not making any sense. Maybe Blue Water Woman is right. Maybe you do just talk to hear yourself speak."

Shakespeare puffed himself up like a riled rooster. "A pox on her and a pox on you. You know very well I wanted to hear about the baby."

"Oh. You know about that? Then why should I need to tell you?" Zach couldn't hold his laughter in any longer.

"I am a cushion and everyone pricks me." Shakespeare reined the mare to go around a boulder. They were in the middle of the valley; the scent of the grass was keen in his nostrils, the sun warm on his cheeks. He felt grand to be alive. "But enough tomfoolery. Be honest with me. How are you taking it?"

Zach never held anything back from McNair. It wouldn't do to try. The oldster had an uncanny knack for seeing right through him. "I made a mess of it at first. I got her all upset because I wasn't sure I was ready to be a father."

"I can't think of anyone more ready. Remember, you are the fruit of your father's loins."

"Thank you for reminding me of that."

"What I meant is that you have root in a fine tree. Your pa is the best man I know. That includes me. You take after him, whether you admit it or not, and you'll be as good a pa as he is."

Zach hoped so. "What do you mean by *best*?"

"I should think it obvious. Not all men are as devoted husbands and fathers as your pa. White or red, a lot of them care more for their horses and their guns than they do for their wives. Or they can't be bothered to spend time with their children because they'd rather be off hunting or fishing or just getting out of the cabin or the lodge." Shakespeare paused. "The true measure of a man isn't in how straight he shoots or how tough he is. The true measure of a man is in his capacity to love. In that regard, your pa beats every gent alive all hollow."

"Capacity to love?" Zach regarded that as an odd standard. But his uncle might have a point. Until he met Louisa, his whole purpose in life was to count coup. Now his purpose in life was her.

"Love is the hardest thing in the world to do right. I'm not talking about giving someone a hug every blue moon and saying you love them. I'm talking about true love, real love. The kind of love you have to work at. The kind where you live for the person you love and not for yourself. The kind where making them happy matters more than your own happiness."

"And you think my pa is that way?"

"Think back. Think of how devoted he is to your ma and your sister and you. Any time you've had a problem, he was right there helping you. He's never set himself above you, never bossed you around like you were—"

"He made me keep my room clean," Zach mentioned.

"Even that was for your own good. Let a child be lazy and they'll be lazy later in life. Mostly he's let you grow true to your nature, and been there to snip and prune when need be."

"You keep comparing me to a plant."

"Because you are. We all are, and when we're young we need the right nurturing. Your pa took care of you just right, and you'll do the same with your own offspring."

Zach drew rein and stared at him.

"What?"

"The things that come out of your mouth never cease to amaze me. If it's not all that silly Bard stuff, it's plants."

"Have a care. Old William S. was never silly. He played with words the way you used to play with those blocks your pa got you. He was—" Shakespeare abruptly stopped.

Zach had held up a hand for silence. Turning, he gazed to the north. "Did you hear that?"

"No. What?"

"I don't know," Zach admitted. "A scream, maybe."

"A scream?" Shakespeare twisted around, his saddle creaking under him, and listened. All he heard was the rustle of the wind and the swish of the mare's tail. "Maybe you imagined it."

"No. I'm pretty sure."

They waited, but the sound wasn't repeated. Zach scowled and reined his bay around. "I think we should go back."

"If they were in trouble, they'd fire shots."

"I still think we should."

"We'd end up wasting most of the morning," Shakespeare replied. "Besides, we haven't seen any sign of hostiles or other whites since those gold-crazy coyotes paid us a visit a while back."

"I know." But Zach wanted to go back anyway. He had an uneasy feeling he didn't like.

"Listen. You just found out your wife is going to have a baby, so naturally you're a little nervous about leaving her alone. We'll look ridiculous, riding all the way back without a reason."

The next instant they had one. From the vicinity of the lake and the women they loved came the crack of a shot.

Blue Water Woman was happy to have some time to herself. She loved McNair dearly, but she needed quiet spells now and then, and with him around it was never quiet. If he wasn't quoting his precious Bard, he was griping about aches in his bones and joints or prattling on about anything and everything under the sun. She'd never met a man, red or white, who talked as much as he did.

Today, after she fed him a breakfast of eggs and potatoes and he rode off, Blue Water Woman took up her knitting and sat in the rocking chair. She loved to knit. Winona had given her the metal needles and taught her the white way, which Winona had learned from Nate. It had surprised Blue Water Woman, a man knowing such a thing. Apparently Nate had learned it from his mother when he was a boy, much to his father's annoyance.

Rocking slowly, Blue Water Woman lost herself in the click of the needles and the intricate weave. She was making Shakespeare what the whites called a sweater. The name puzzled her. Sweaters were usually worn in cold weather, when people sweated least. She thought it made more sense for whites to call it a warmer, but then, the whites did and said many things that to this day perplexed her.

Blue Water Woman sometimes marveled that she had wed a white man. The Flatheads didn't hate the whites, as the Blackfeet and some other tribes did, but few took white mates.

She remembered when they first met. Back then he'd had brown hair and he didn't quote the Bard every time he opened his mouth. Truth was, he'd been shy and quiet—as incredible as that was to believe—but he'd had the same wonderful personality. The one thing he did then that he still did now was love to laugh, and that laugh of his was infectious. When Shakespeare laughed, the whole world laughed with him.

He was handsome, too. Age had changed his features, as it did everyone's. Now he had more lines on his face, but his eyes held the same twinkle. To her he was the handsomest man alive. She would never tell him that, of course. He would boast of it forever.

It was a mystery, love. Part of it was plain to understand; two people met, they were attracted, they wanted to be together. But another part, the deeper part, was a mystery to her people and, she had found, to the whites, as well. It was fine to say that love happened when one heart reached out to another. But why that particular heart out of all the hearts in the world?

Blue Water Woman stopped knitting and chuckled. Here she was, thinking thoughts more fitting for a girl who had seen but sixteen winters.

The sitting had made her stiff. She got up, put

her knitting on the rocking chair, and went out. She took her rifle, as she always did, and strolled to the lake. A haze hung over it, as was common in the summer.

The lake teemed with water birds. She liked to watch them swim and dive. She particularly liked the couples, and the mothers with their little ones.

Blue Water Woman regretted not being able to give McNair children. She'd told him she didn't, but she did. Had they wed when they were young, she would have delighted in having babies until she couldn't have had them anymore.

Blue Water Woman stretched. She gazed across the lake, toward Zach and Lou's cabin, barely visible on the far side. She thought she saw two people come out. One had to be Louisa; she was wearing a dress, unusual for her, as Lou preferred buckskins. The other figure was a man—and he appeared to be pushing Lou ahead of him.

Blue Water Woman blinked, and the pair were gone around a corner. She moved to her left to try and see them again, but couldn't. Alarm spiked through her. The man couldn't be Zach. Zach was off with Shakespeare. And anyway, Zach would never push Lou, not for any reason.

She told herself she must be mistaken. There had been no sign of strangers in the valley. But she couldn't deny her own eyes. Quickly, she hurried to the corral and brought out her dun. She didn't bother with a saddle. She had no need of one; she had been riding bareback since she was old enough to straddle a horse.

Mounting, Blue Water Woman jabbed her heels and brought the dun to a gallop. The wind on her

face and in her hair felt nice. She glanced to the
north, but she still couldn't see the two figures.

It was a long way from her cabin to Lou's. She
passed Nate and Winona's at the west end, and
then flew along the north shore until she reined
up in a swirl of dust.

The front door was wide open.

Alighting, Blue Water Woman leveled her
Hawken. "Louisa? Are you in there?" When she got
no answer, she warily stepped to the doorway.

Inside, it was neat and tidy, as Lou always kept
it. Pans and a bowl were on the counter. Nothing
looked out of place. Blue Water Woman saw no
signs of a struggle. She saw Lou's rifle propped
near the door. That puzzled her. If Lou had been
taken by hostiles, they would surely have taken
it. Guns were as highly prized as horses.

Blue Water Woman went around the corner.
The thick woodland that bordered the lake was
an unbroken wall of green.

"Louisa! Where are you?"

Again, no answer.

Her dread climbing, Blue Water Woman shouted
several more times. When she still got no response,
she came to a decision. She moved to the water's
edge, raised her rifle over her head, and fired.
The shot would carry a long way. Shakespeare
and Zach had not been gone that long. They were
bound to hear it and fly back.

Blue Water Woman reloaded. She debated
whether to stay and wait for them or to go after
Lou by herself. She really had no choice. Lou must
be in trouble. The more time that went by, the
greater the chance that whoever took Lou would
get away.

Blue Water Woman climbed back on the dun. She reined toward the forest. Once more she called out to Lou. The silence preyed on her nerves. It was *too* quiet. All the birds, the squirrels, everything had gone silent. A bad omen. She wished Nate and Winona were home. She could use their help. Indeed, whoever took Lou would find her father-in-law a formidable adversary. Nate King was a superb tracker and a skilled fighter.

His son was a holy terror.

Blue Water Woman imagined that Zach would be beside himself. It wouldn't surprise her if when Zach caught whoever took Lou—and Zach *would* catch him—he chopped the man into bits and pieces. Blue Water Woman cared for Zach, cared for him dearly, but there had been times, especially when he was younger, that he worried her. When his blood was up he was a rabid wolf.

Off in the trees, something moved.

She drew rein, tucked her rifle to her shoulder, and put her thumb on the hammer. But whatever she saw was gone. It might have been a deer. She waited, and when the woods stayed still, she lowered the Hawken and rode on.

Shadows dappled her and turned the vegetation into a patchwork quilt of light and dark. It played tricks on the eyes. Twice she thought she saw a two-legged shape silhouetted against the green, but either it vanished or it was never really there.

Blue Water Woman didn't realize her mouth had gone dry until she tried to swallow. The clomp of the dun's hooves was the only sound. She looked every which way so she wouldn't be taken by surprise, and soon had a crick in her neck. She willed herself to stay calm and shut her worry from her mind. She must stay focused on one thing and one thing only.

A patch of white appeared. Then others, mixed with patches of brown. It took a few seconds for Blue Water Woman to recognize them for what they were—the coat of a pinto. She drew rein.

The pinto was just standing there, head bowed, dozing.

Blue Water Woman looked all around. She swung her leg over the dun and slid down. The pinto must belong to whoever had taken Lou, but where were they? She slowly advanced. As quietly as she could, she cocked the Hawken. Passing under a pine, she paused to scour the undergrowth.

A sound reached her. A low cry, muffled. She tried to pinpoint where it came from. When she heard it again, she moved cautiously. She went around a thicket—and saw Lou.

Louisa was on her side, bound wrists and ankles. She had been gagged with a piece of her dress. Her eyes were wide and she began to shake her head and thrash about.

Blue Water Woman saw no one else. She hastened to her friend, whispering, "Don't worry. I will cut you free."

Lou thrashed harder.

Blue Water Woman took her finger from the Hawken's trigger and put her hand on the hilt of her knife. She heard rustling and started to turn. She wasn't quite all the way around when a blow to her head sent her stumbling to her knees. Pain exploded. She looked up.

A warrior was poised with a large rock in his hand.

"No," Blue Water Woman said.

The world faded to black.

Chapter Seven

Louisa King thought she was done for when the warrior gripped her by the throat and raised his knife. But instead of stabbing her, he shoved her toward the front door and came after her, pushing her when she didn't move fast enough to suit him. She almost made a grab for her rifle. The jab of his blade low in her back dissuaded her.

Lou blinked in the sudden glare of the sun and paused. He pushed her again, toward the corner. She thought he might want her to mount her horse, but then he pushed her toward the woods.

"I'll do what you want. There's no need to keep shoving me," Lou said, even thought she knew it was a waste of breath. She glanced at him and saw that he had taken Zach's rope from its peg on the wall and brought it along.

The Outcast pushed her again. He was mad at himself and taking it out on her. He didn't need her alive, but she was still breathing. It was the first weakness he had shown since the day that changed his world. He could remedy that by plunging his knife between her shoulder blades, but he thought of her belly, and couldn't.

Lou would dearly love to know what his intentions were. To her knowledge, Indians rarely committed rape. Small comfort at best, since there were so many worse things they did. Mutilating enemies was common, and some tribes enjoyed torture. She prayed to God her captor wasn't from one of them.

The Outcast paused at the tree line to look back. He gazed across the lake, and was taken aback to see a figure moving along the far shore. A woman, it looked like, and she was facing him. It had to be the Flathead.

Lou halted. She wondered why he had stopped. Having second thoughts, she hoped. But no, he shoved her again and barked at her in his own tongue, no doubt telling her to keep going.

The Outcast had seen the Flathead run toward her lodge. Either she was going for help or for a horse. Either way, she threatened to spoil everything.

Lou trudged angrily along. She was more mad at herself than the warrior; he was only doing what was natural. No, she was mad at herself for leaving the front door open and not keeping her rifle or pistols within easy reach. Most of all, she was mad because her carelessness might prove costly for the people she loved most in the world. They were bound to come after her, and her captor did not strike her as the type to die easily.

The Outcast was debating what to do. The important thing was to get away unnoticed. The woman across the lake might spoil that.

Lou tripped over a root and nearly fell. Her dress kept getting snagged on brush and limbs.

She'd pull it loose, only to have it catch again ten steps later. She vowed that from here on out, she would only wear buckskins.

A whinny didn't surprise her. She'd figured that the warrior had a horse. Few entered King Valley on foot. It was too remote, too far from the trails used by whites and red men alike. She rounded a thicket and beheld a pinto. A fine animal, if she was any judge. She seemed to remember Zach saying that some Indians were partial to pintos over all others. It had something to do with the bright colors, which Indians loved.

Her captor jabbed her in the back to get her attention, then motioned at the ground.

Lou gathered that he wanted her to sit. She did, and was roughly pushed onto her back. For a few anxious moments she feared her notion about being raped was wrong; but no, he made her lie on her side with her arms behind her, and he proceeded to cut short lengths from Zach's rope to bind her ankles and wrists. She didn't like it, but there was nothing she could do. She noticed that while he bound her tight, he didn't do it so tight that the rope cut into her flesh. Then he reached for the hem of her dress.

"No!" Lou instinctively bleated, and the razor point of his knife flashed at her throat. All he did was prick her. A warning, she reckoned, and watched as he cut two strips. "Dang you. I sent all the way to St. Louis for this, and look at what you've done."

Her anger puzzled the Outcast. Most women would be groveling in fear. But not this one. She was white, and she was an enemy, but she was

gloriously brave. He caught himself and frowned.
Gripping her jaw, he motioned for her to open her
mouth.

Lou balked. It was bad enough being tied. But
when he poked her in the ribs with that long
blade of his, she did as he wanted, and the next
moment her mouth was filled with a piece of her
dress. "Wonderful," she said, only it came out as
"Unerful."

The Outcast tied the other strip over her mouth
so she couldn't spit out the gag. Rising, he faced
their back trail. In the distance hooves drummed.
He went around the thicket until he was out of
sight of the woman. Crouching, he wormed his
way into it until he could see her without her seeing him.

Lou wondered where he had gotten to. She tried
to rub off the strip over her mouth. Failing, she
went to sit up and froze. Someone was calling her
name. With a start, she recognized Blue Water
Woman's voice. She tried to yell, but the gag muffled her cries.

Blue Water Woman stopped shouting.

Lou wriggled toward the lake. She figured her
friend was wondering where she had got to. Blue
Water Woman wouldn't know what had happened
and might turn around and go back to her own
cabin.

Then, to Lou's relief, she saw her. Blue Water
Woman, her rifle at the ready. Lou almost laughed
for joy. She wanted to scream for Blue Water Woman
to hurry and cut her free before the warrior came
back. Her friend glided past the thicket—and a
figure rose out of its depths.

Frantic, Lou shook her head and thrashed about, trying to warn Blue Water Woman before it was too late. She watched, aghast, as the warrior picked up a rock. Blue Water Woman started to turn. Lou thrashed harder but stopped at the thud of the blow.

Blue Water Woman fell to her knees. The warrior raised the rock to hit her again, but she pitched to the ground, unconscious.

The warrior threw the rock aside.

Relief washed over Lou, but it was short-lived. The next moment the warrior had her in his arms and threw her over the pinto. He swung up and lashed the reins.

She was being abducted.

From the heights to the west, the valley was a green gem rich with life, the lake blue turquoise at its middle.

The seven Tun-kua gazed down at the brown dots that were the lodges of the invaders.

"We still have a long way to go," Splashes Blood said.

Skin Shredder grunted and continued their descent. He did not care how far it was. He had come to avenge the death of his brother and nothing would stop him, save his own end.

They passed through ranks of tall firs, somber with shadows, and came on a grassy shelf and a spring. Skin Shredder hardly gave it a glance and was halfway across the shelf when Splashes Blood cleared his throat.

"We walked all day and we walked all night and now you would have us deny our dry throats?"

Skin Shredder stopped. "Drink if you want."

"We have not eaten, either."

"You have your deer meat."

All of them had bundles of dried venison, which six of them now unwrapped. Splashes Blood bit into a piece and smacked his lips. "You are not eating."

"I am not hungry." Skin Shredder began to pace, his gaze on the lake and the lodges.

"You think of one thing and one thing only. It is not good."

"When I want someone to tell me how I should think, I will ask them."

Splashes Blood stopped chewing and frowned. "We have been friends since our mothers took us from our cradleboards, yet you talk to me with so little respect."

Skin Shredder stopped pacing. He frowned, too, and then raised a hand to the scarred ridges on his face. "I am sorry. Killing the Bear People is all I have thought of for many sleeps now. I want them to suffer. I want them to suffer more than anything."

"They killed my brother, too," Splashes Blood reminded him. "We must not underestimate them. We must be rested and have our wits about us."

"It is hard to rest when your heart burns with the need to slay."

"You must try," Splashes Blood insisted.

Skin Shredder slung his bow across his back. His meat was tied by a deerskin thong to his wolf hide belt. All of them wore such belts.

The Tun-kua rite of manhood required three things of every warrior: that he scar his face with the symbols of their clan; that he fast for five days and five sleeps and have a vision; and that he hunt and slay a wolf and forever wear its hide.

"I have been told there is a girl among the Bear People," Splashes Blood mentioned. "Those who have seen her say she looks to be but fifteen winters."

"You and your girls . . ." Skin Shredder sank his teeth into a piece of meat. "Maybe the Bear People do not age as we do. Maybe they look younger than they are."

"No matter how old she is, I want her first."

"You can have her. I want only to spill blood. The rest does not interest me as it once did."

Another warrior had moved to where the shelf fell away into pines. He now pointed and called out to the others. "Come see. I do not know what it is, but it was not there the last time I spied on them."

Skin Shredder and Splashes Blood went over.

"Where is this thing, Star Dancer?"

"Look at the east end of the lake, close to the trees. I think it is a lodge. But it is not like the other lodges. It is longer and round at the top."

"I see it," Splashes Blood said.

"It is too far to tell much," Skin Shredder declared. "But you are right. It is different from the others."

"What can it mean? Have more Bear People come? Or have other people come to the valley?"

The question caused Skin Shredder to clench his fists. "It is as it was by the bay. First a few came, and then more and more, until we were driven from our home."

"The world has too many people."

"Will we move again?" Star Dancer asked.

"No." Skin Shredder was emphatic. "This time we will not let them drive us off. This time we kill them as they come."

"But if they come in great numbers . . ." Splashes Blood did not say the rest. They all knew his meaning.

Skin Shredder gloomily ate. That was the problem. The Tun-kua were a small tribe. Never had there been more than several hundred of them, and since being forced from their home, their numbers had dwindled. Battles with other tribes, wild beasts, and disease had taken a toll. "They are not in great numbers now. We will kill all those who are here and burn their lodges as a warning to any who come later."

"And if some come anyway and stay?"

"We will kill them, too. We will be ghosts in the night and stalkers by day, and they will fear us. We might even let some of them leave to tell the rest of their kind that this valley is bad medicine."

"I like that idea. Fear is more powerful than blood. Fear will keep them away. Spilling their blood will only make them mad and they will want vengeance." Splashes Blood grimly smiled. "Look at us."

"Fear is good," Star Dancer agreed.

"We will talk it over with the Old One when we return to our village," Skin Shredder proposed. "He is wise in all things and will help guide our steps."

Refreshed by the meat and the water, they were soon under way. Skin Shredder was in the lead, studying landmarks. To the north gleamed a glacier high atop a mountain. To the south was a cleft peak. To the east, barely visible on the far valley rim, was the gap that led out of the valley into the world beyond.

Splashes Blood cleared his throat. "I have been thinking. We should not burn everything."

"No?"

"They have many wondrous things, these Bear People. They have thunder sticks that spew fire and death. They have knives made of a new kind of metal. They have blankets much finer than ours, and who knows what else in their lodges."

"The Bear People own much that we do not."

"What is to stop us from owning it? After we kill them, why not take all that we want?"

"It will not be much," Skin Shredder noted. "We can take only what we can carry."

"We can take a lot if we pack it on their horses."

Here was a thought that excited Skin Shredder. The Tun-kua never had horses of their own. It put them at a great disadvantage when waging war and in moving about.

Star Dancer said to Splashes Blood, "It is a fine idea. I am for it."

"But we do not know how to handle horses," Skin Shredder reminded them.

"If the Bear People learned, we can learn."

"They are animals and we are men," Star Dancer declared.

"It will be a great thing we do," Splashes Blood said. "Our people will praise us. Songs will be sung around the campfires about what we have done."

Skin Shredder tingled with excitement. It was a very fine idea, indeed. He couldn't wait to start the slaying. Not only would he have his revenge, he stood to stand high in the councils of the Tun-kua. "We should thank the Bear People before we kill them." And he did something he rarely did—he smiled.

Chapter Eight

Zach King tried to tell himself he had no reason to worry. There had been only the one shot. If Lou and Blue Water Woman were beset by hostiles, surely there would have been more. They were tough, strong women; they wouldn't go down without a fight.

Then Zach remembered that his wife was forever traipsing outside without her weapons and leaving the front door open. He glanced at McNair, riding hard beside him, and said loud enough to be heard over the pounding of hooves, "What do you think?"

Shakespeare thought they were making a mountain out of a prairie dog mound. There could be a perfectly ordinary explanation for the shot. Either woman might have shot a deer or some other animal for the cook pot. Or maybe a fox had got in with the chickens. Or a rattlesnake decided to sun itself close to one of their cabins. He seemed to recollect that Louisa, in particular, was skittish about snakes.

Since Zach was looking at him and waiting for a reply, Shakespeare shrugged and said, "I bet they're fine, but it doesn't hurt to check." He said that last for Zach's benefit. The boy—Shakespeare mentally caught himself—the young man had a tendency to overreact. When there really was danger, well, heaven help anyone or anything that threatened Zach King or those he cared for.

The south shore came into sight. There stood McNair's cabin, awash in sunlight, as picturesque as a painting.

Shakespeare counted the horses in his corral. "My wife went somewhere on her dun." That the packhorses were still there told him that no one had stolen it. No self-respecting horse thief would steal just one animal.

Zach rose in the stirrups to try and see the north shore. He spied his chimney. It was too far to be certain, but he thought wisps of smoke curled to the sky. That was a good sign. Lou was supposed to be doing some baking. "Do we stop at your place or go on to mine?"

"On to yours."

When they reached the west end of the lake, Zach slowed to a walk to spare their sweaty mounts. "If they ask why we came back, I'll tell them I forgot my whetstone."

"'You do advance your cunning more and more,'" Shakespeare quoted.

"I just don't want Lou to think that I think she can't take care of herself. She'd never let me hear the end of it."

Shakespeare chuckled. "'Oh, what men dare do. What men may do. What men daily do, not knowing what they do.'"

"Can you say that in English or Shoshone so I can understand it?"

"Lout," Shakespeare said. "It's not my fault

you're so light of brain." He quoted again. " 'A lip of much contempt speeds from me.' "

Zach laughed, but his heart wasn't in their banter. He'd noticed that the front door to their cabin was wide open. "Why don't women ever listen?"

"That was a rhetorical question, I trust."

"A what?"

"Women are the queens of curds and creams, and queens need not stoop to listening to their subjects."

"I ask a serious question and that's the answer I get?"

"Haven't you learned by now that women have minds of their own? They listen when it suits them and don't when it doesn't. But to be fair, men don't listen at all."

"What are you talking about? I listen to Lou all the time."

"You only pretend you do. When she talks about cooking and sewing and all the things she does, you think about hunting and fishing and the black powder you need to buy the next time you're at Bent's Fort. When she goes on about how you need to repair the roof, you think about going for a ride up in the mountains." Shakespeare chuckled. "We nod our heads and say 'Yes, dear,' and they let us cuddle with them at night. Not a bad trade, if I say so myself."

"I don't do any of that."

"You don't? Then someone else is the father of Lou's child? My word. Who can it be?"

A retort leaped to the tip of Zach's tongue, but then he noticed something else. "I don't see your dun anywhere."

"You don't?" Shakespeare had assumed his

wife was paying Lou a visit. "We'll ask Lou if she's seen her."

The quiet, the smoke rising from the chimney, had eased much of Zach's concern. He was annoyed more than anything, rankled that Lou had left the front door open yet again. Fifty yards out, he suddenly drew rein. "I'm going to teach my wife a lesson. Stay with the horses."

"Are you sure that's wise? Why stir the hornets when they're being peaceable?"

"There's only one hornet, and its high time she learned that leaving that door open could get her in trouble someday." Zach handed the reins over and turned to jog to the cabin.

"Be gentle, son," Shakespeare cautioned.

Making no more sound than the wind, Zach gave the chicken coop a wide berth so he wouldn't set the hens to clucking. He came to the front wall and crouched. Grinning, he cat-stepped to the open door. It would serve Lou right, his scaring her silly. Taking a deep breath, he bounded inside while simultaneously giving voice to a roar worthy of a grizzly.

No one was there.

Scratching his head, Zach backed out. He beckoned to McNair, then scoured the shore and the forest.

Shakespeare didn't need to ask what had happened. He was off the mare before it came to a stop. "Maybe we should fire a few shots in the air. It'll bring them on the run."

"Good idea." Zach went to raise his rifle, then froze. "God in heaven," he breathed.

Shakespeare turned, and thought his heart would burst in his chest.

From out of the woods, her face smeared with blood, staggered Blue Water Woman.

Louisa King had felt overwhelming fear before. There was the time Zach was nearly killed by a grizzly; the time the army took him into custody and he was put on trial for murder; the time a wolverine tried to kill them. Other instances came to mind. She should have been used to it, but she wasn't. The fear that gripped her as she was being carried off by the warrior who had invaded their valley chilled her to the marrow.

Lou knew that Zach and Shakespeare would be gone for most of the day. She couldn't count on rescue from them. She had seen Blue Water Woman brutally struck with a rock, had seen her friend collapse and blood stream over her brow and face, and felt certain she was dead. With Nate and Winona gone, and the Nansusequa off after buffalo, there was no one to come to her rescue.

Her only hope was that Zach could track her captor down. But if Zach and Shakespeare didn't get back until dark, they'd have to wait until morning to come after her, unless they used torches. By then she would be miles away.

Presently the warrior came to a stream fed by a glacier.

Lou held her breath. Would he cross it or use it to hide his tracks?

The Outcast drew rein in the middle of the stream and shifted to look behind him. He grunted in satisfaction. There was no sign of pursuit yet. He rode up the stream toward the mountains, counting on the swift-flowing water to wash away most of the pinto's prints. Most, but not all.

Lou's heart sank. This was exactly what she dreaded. Now Zach and Shakespeare would have a harder time finding her. She closed her eyes and smothered a slight tremble. Ordinarily she was as brave as the next woman, but she was in dire straits. She figured the warrior was taking her to his village, where she would spend the rest of her days as his blanket warmer.

Like hell. Lou would slit her wrists before letting another man touch her. But then she thought of the new life taking shape within her, and her eyes moistened as she realized that she didn't have it in her to do away with herself if it meant doing away with the baby, too.

The Outcast studied his captive. He was impressed by how quiet she was. Most woman would scream or be hysterical. This little one, he mused, had exceptional courage. It reminded him of *her.* Again pain filled him. Not physical pain, but the deep searing pain of raw emotion. It occurred to him that he had thought of her more since he came across this young white woman than he had in many moons.

The Outcast told himself his feelings were to be expected. Such a loss, the loss of someone who meant everything, someone loved and adored and cherished beyond all others, could never be forgotten. The best he could do, the best any person could do, was to hold the hurt at bay by piling rocks of denial around his heart so that the hurt could not touch it. The problem, of course, was that piles of rocks always had gaps in them, thin gaps, yes, but gaps where a stray feeling or an unguarded thought could slip through.

A tiny voice in the Outcast's mind told him to

spare himself the misery. All he had to do was draw his knife and slit the white woman's throat. One slash and her life was over. One slash and his hurt was banished. He placed his hand on the hilt.

Lou opened her eyes and looked at her captor. She wished she spoke his tongue or he spoke hers. She would beg him to set her free so she could go back to her home and to those she loved most in the world. She saw him give a slight start, and wondered why.

The Outcast was about to draw his knife when his captive fixed her eyes on him. Such remarkable eyes, as blue as the lake. Mute appeal was mirrored in their depths. An appeal so potent, it caught him about his heart with a pelt of the softest fur. His head swirled, and he hissed in annoyance. "Stop looking at me," he said, but she didn't understand him and kept on doing it. He raised his hand to smack her.

Lou turned away. She wondered why he was so mad. It didn't bode well. Men prone to get angry were also often violent. He might beat her if she wasn't careful. In despair she sagged across the pinto, her cheek against its side. Her belly was starting to hurt, and that worried her. It couldn't be good for her to be over the horse this way.

She gazed off through the trees, longing for a glimpse of her cabin, but they had come too far to the west. Soon, they would start to climb into the high country. It puzzled her. The only way out of the valley, as far as she knew, was to the east. Why was her captor heading west?

The Outcast scanned the valley rim. To the

northwest was the glacier. To the south were peaks so high, they brushed the clouds. Ahead, to the west, were forested slopes that rose in tiers to rocky ramparts. He would set his traps there.

Inwardly, the Outcast smiled. Killing the breed and the old white man would take his mind off *her*. He had a lot to do and he might as well start now. Reining out of the stream and up the bank, he came to a stop at a stand of saplings and slid down. The saplings were ideal for what he had in mind.

Lou raised her head. Hope flared anew. She'd figured he would stay in the stream for miles. That was the smart thing to do if he wanted to shake off pursuit. She saw him take the rope and cut a couple of short lengths. Then he moved off into the undergrowth.

He had left her alone.

Instantly, Lou shifted to try to slide off the pinto. But her legs were partly numb and she couldn't quite manage it. Suddenly her captor was back. He had a downed tree limb, which he broke into pieces. Each piece was no thicker than his middle finger. One was about a foot long, the other six inches, the third even shorter. As she watched, he sat and drew his knife and started cutting on first one and then the other.

Lou would have to wait for another chance to try to escape. Curious what he was up to, she watched him intently.

The Outcast sharpened the sticks. At the opposite ends of the long one and the short one he cut notches. A rock served to pound the long stick into the ground. Stepping to a thin sapling he had chosen, the Outcast reached overhead and climbed. He used only his arms. Under his weight the tree began to bend. As it bent, his feet sank lower and lower until they were on the ground again. The sapling was now curved like a bow.

The Outcast tied one end of the rope to the sapling, about a third of the way from the top. Holding the rope securely so the tree couldn't snap back up, he tied the other end of the rope to the short stick, then knelt beside the stake.

Horror gripped Lou. She had divined what he was up to. Zach and Nate used the same trick to kill rabbits and the like. "God, no!" she exclaimed through her gag.

The Outcast glanced at her.

"Why are you doing this?" Lou struggled against her bonds.

The Outcast patted the sapling. He didn't understand a word the woman was saying, but he understood the worry on her face. "I do what I must. You and your man and your friends are my enemies."

The Outcast aligned the notch in the short stick with the notch in the stake, setting them so the short stick would release if it was bumped. Rising, he took the third sharpened stick and carefully tied it to the bent sapling at the height of a mounted man. He cast about until he found pine limbs that suited his purpose and set them so they hid the rope and the stake. Now all that was needed was for one of his pursuers to ride by and jar the limb that hid the short stick. The sapling would whip up and impale the rider.

Lou's mouth went dry. She had realized the

awful truth. He wasn't taking her to his village. He had no interest in her other than as bait. He was using her to lure Zach and Shakespeare to their deaths.

Chapter Nine

Shakespeare McNair was in a simmering rage. At his age it wasn't often that his emotions ran out of control, but the horrid sight of his devoted wife staggering out of the forest with blood oozing down her forehead and over her face tore a screech of pure fury from Shakespeare's throat.

Zach was younger by more than fifty years and considered fleet of foot, but it was Shakespeare who reached Blue Water Woman first, Shakespeare who caught her as she collapsed, Shakespeare who gently lowered her to the ground and tenderly touched her cheek.

"God, no."

Zach hunkered on the other side of her. "How bad is she?" he asked.

Shakespeare was probing with his fingertips to find out. She had been struck; that much was obvious. He found a deep gash above her hairline. It was the only wound, but it was enough. The blood would not stop. "We must get her inside."

"I'll help." Zach was near frantic about Lou, but Blue Water Woman needed immediate attention.

They carried her into the cabin. Zach was all for putting her on the bed, but Shakespeare set her down on the bearskin rug in front of the stone fireplace. Zach brought a washcloth and Shakespeare pressed it to the wound to stanch the flow.

"Water, son. Hot water, as quick as you can."

"Leave it to me."

Shakespeare bent and whispered, "Precious? Can you hear me? It's your Snowball." Those were the endearments they used most when they cuddled.

Blue Water Woman's eyelids fluttered. Her eyes opened but didn't stay open. She weakly stirred and managed to say, "Husband? Is that you? I hurt so much."

Shakespeare clasped her hand in both of his. A lump clogged his throat and he could barely see her for his tears. "I'll take care of you, don't you worry. I'll tend you and bandage you and get you to our cabin."

"Lou," Blue Water Woman said.

"What about her?"

"She's been taken. I saw her tied and gagged." Blue Water Woman found it hard to think. "I saw who took her."

"How many are there?"

"One."

"That's all?" Shakespeare was relieved. He'd imagined an entire war party. "Zach will head out after them in a just a bit. Don't you worry. He'll find them and bring her back."

Blue Water Woman licked her lips. So simple an act, yet it took all her strength. "Shakespeare?"

"Don't talk. Lie still. You need to rest."

Struggling to stay conscious, Blue Water Woman got out, "This is important. The warrior who took Lou . . ."

"What about him?"

"He is a Blood."

Shakespeare was surprised. The Bloods were part of what the whites called the Blackfoot Confederacy, an alliance had that controlled the northern plains and parts of southern Canada since long before Lewis and Clark. The three principal tribes were the Blackfeet, the Piegans, and the Bloods—at least those were the names the whites gave them. Their real names, the names by which they called themselves, were the Siksika, the Piikani, and the Kainai.

The Bloods—or Kainai—were so called because of the habit they had of rubbing red ochre on their faces. They were a proud, fearless people, fiercely protective of their land. Shakespeare had had dealings with them in the past, before they came to distrust and dislike the white man and drove all whites from their land or slew them.

Shakespeare scratched his beard, pondering. King Valley was far from their usual haunts. Bloods hardly ever ventured this deep into the mountains. For a lone warrior to be there was unthinkable; there had to be more. He reasoned that the Blood his wife had seen must be part of a larger war party.

"Husband?"

"I'm here." Shakespeare squeezed her hand and kissed her on the cheek, not caring one whit that he got her blood on his lips.

"I am tired," Blue Water Woman said. In truth, she had never felt so weak, so drained.

"You've lost a lot of blood, but you should be all right in a few days," Shakespeare predicted. He was sugarcoating her condition to put her at ease.

Truth was, she might have internal bleeding. Or, worse, the gash was deeper than it seemed, and the force of the blow had driven bone fragments into her brain.

"If you do not mind, I will sleep now." Blue Water Woman closed her eyes and a dark mist enveloped her.

Zach came hurrying over. "I kindled the fire and have water on. I can't stay any longer."

Shakespeare nodded. "Off you go, then. But you should know: Lou is still alive. She's been taken by the Bloods."

A hot sensation spread from Zach's neck to the top of his head. "I'll count coup on all of them."

"Blue Water Woman saw only one, but there must be more." Shakespeare snagged Zach's sleeve as Zach turned. "Be careful. The Bloods are good fighters and damn clever. They'll be expecting someone to come after them. They'll be ready."

"They won't be ready for me," Zach vowed, and ran out the door in long lopes.

Shakespeare listened to the drum of hooves fade. By rights he should be with the boy, watching his back. But he couldn't leave Blue Water Woman. Not with her like this. He tenderly touched her chin and leaned down to whisper in her ear. "Don't you die on me. You hear? You're the love of my life. Our hearts are entwined forever." He coughed and blinked, and tears trickled down his cheeks. A low moan escaped him.

Shakespeare broke down and sobbed.

The Tun-kua descended the slope with the agility of mountain goats and the stamina of Apaches. Powerfully built, their short, muscular bodies lent them superb endurance. They could jog half a day without tiring. This served them well now, as it was a long way from the top of the mountain to the bottom, many leagues of steep slopes and thick woods.

Skin Shredder pushed to descend as low as they could before the sun went down.

They took infrequent rests. When they came to a ridge that afforded a sweeping view of the valley, Skin Shredder raised an arm and the other warriors stopped. Some took out their food bundles to eat. Others gazed about the pristine wonderland, marveling at the abundance of wildlife. Their own valley had much to recommend it, but this valley, the Valley of the Bear People, as they had come to call it of late, was a paradise.

Black-capped chickadees played in the thickets. Grosbeaks frolicked in the pines. Red crossbills winged through the air bobbing their heads and uttering their strange cry of *beep-beep-beep*. Hummingbirds whizzed and dived. Flocks of small pine siskin flew from stand to stand. Gorgeous tanagers stared at them from high limbs. Jays squawked noisily. Black-and-white magpies added their calls to the chorus.

The evidence of mammals was everywhere. Tracks of elk and shaggy mountain buffalo. The weasel called the valley home. So did the mink and the marten. Mountain sheep could be seen on the heights. Badger burrows dotted open slopes. In the waterways beaver thrived, and in the largest stream, otter. Noisy squirrels sat on pine limbs, chewing nuts. Others scampered about the ground. Chipmunks would run in fright with their tails high.

There was sign of meat eaters, too. Bear, mountain lion, bobcat. Wolves and foxes. Coyotes were especially numerous.

Back when the Tun-kua first came to the mountains, the tribe was delighted when they discovered the valley. It had everything they could want. They'd camped by the lake and held council. Everyone agreed it should be their new home.

But the next day something huge stirred the waters of the lake. All of them saw the water roil, saw a giant form swim just below the surface. A water devil, the older among them called it. Bad medicine.

The second night they heard strange cries. Not the howl of wolves or the yip of coyotes, but ululating wails and fierce roars from the vicinity of the glacier, borne to them by the wind. It filled them with unease. More bad medicine.

The morning of the third day dawned bright and beautiful until it was learned that one of their number was missing. A woman had gone into the forest to gather firewood and hadn't returned. A search was conducted, with every warrior taking part. The best trackers among them were able to follow her tracks into the woods as far as a small clearing, where they abruptly stopped. There they also found other tracks, huge tracks, tracks unlike any bear but vaguely bearlike, tracks with long claws and narrow heels. The story the tracks told was plain. The woman had entered the clearing and the thing that made the huge tracks rushed out at her. She never got off a cry. Drops of blood told them they would never see her again.

This was the worst medicine of all. Another council was held and this time the tribe decided to move on. It was with reluctance that they climbed the west slopes and filed through a pass into the valley beyond. This other valley proved to be almost as bountiful. There was no lake—but no mysterious water creature, either. There was no glacier—but the nights were not disturbed by hideous cries. Best of all, they stayed there a week and no one disappeared. It became their new home.

Now, gazing out over the blue of the lake and the green of the valley bottom, Skin Shredder almost wished that this valley was their home. From time to time warriors had ventured here to hunt and fish, but they never stayed more than a few sleeps. The cries from the glacier and the roiling of the lake water always reminded them it was the haunt of creatures better left undisturbed. Creatures from when the world was young.

The Tun-kua believed that at one time the earth had been filled with animals unlike any they were familiar with. Huge creatures, many covered with thick hair, creatures that dwarfed even the elk and the buffalo. Cats with teeth as long as a man's arm. Bears that could reach the tops of trees. Four-legged giants with two tails, one at each end, and two teeth, each as long as a canoe.

Tun-kua legend had it that most of these creatures had died out. But not all of them. The same with the red-haired cannibals, once so numerous and the scourge of tribes everywhere. The Tun-kua also passed down tales of the little people who once lived in the hills near the bay but retreated into the interior when the tribes grew in number.

Skin Shredder thought of all of this as he stood staring across the valley.

"You should eat," Splashes Blood said, breaking into his reverie.

"I am not hungry."

"We have far to go yet before dark."

"Are you my friend or my mother?"

Splashes Blood chewed and shrugged. "It is your stomach. If you like it empty, that is your choice." He gazed at the lake. "Have you noticed their wood lodges?"

"What about them?"

"Usually there is smoke rising from all of them. Today smoke rises from only one."

"You think only a few of the Bear People are there?"

"It could be. We know they go out of the valley to the east from time to time. Where they go, we cannot say. But they always come back."

"Just so there are some for us to kill," Skin Shredder said. "I will spill their blood for the blood of my brother."

"If I am right, if some of their lodges are empty, we can take whatever we want."

Skin Shredder had been thinking the same thing. "Their lodges are not like ours. We have watched, and they do not go in and out as we do. Their lodges do not have flaps. Part of the wood opens and closes. How is a mystery."

"They are people, like us. What they can do, we can do."

"They are not like us," Skin Shredder disagreed. "Their bodies are different; their ways are different."

"I am only saying that we are as smart as they are. What they have figured out, we can figure out."

Star Dancer joined them. He raised an arm and pointed. "When you are done arguing, look there."

Skin Shredder tingled with excitement. Midway between the ridge and the valley floor a rider had appeared. A man on a black-and-white horse, climbing an open slope.

"He is not white," Splashes Blood observed.

"He is still an enemy."

"There is a woman with him," Star Dancer said. "She is on her belly over the horse."

Skin Shredder peered intently. He never ceased to be amazed at how sharp Star Dancer's eyes were. A human hawk, Star Dancer. But he was right. There *was* a woman. A white woman.

"See how her arms are behind her back? And her feet are close together? She is tied. I think she is gagged, too, but it is too far for me to be sure."

"Tied and gagged?" Splashes Blood mused. "That warrior has stolen her from the Bear Men."

A smile curled the corners of Skin Shredder's mouth. "What he has stolen from them, we can steal from him." He motioned at the others. "Come, brothers. Tonight we eat two hearts."

Seven human wolves bounded down the ridge, their scarred faces lit with the glow of bloodlust.

Chapter Ten

Zach King had a temper.

He'd had it since he was old enough to remember. When he got mad, he got *really* mad, so mad that he sometimes lost control and did things he later regretted. In a few instances he had gone berserk.

His father and mother always cautioned him that if he wasn't careful, one day his temper would get him into trouble. They were right. He ended up being put on trial and nearly hanged.

Since meeting Lou, Zach had tried extra hard to keep his temper under control. He got angry, sure, but these days he rarely became so mad that he was beside himself with fury.

This day was one of them.

As Zach tracked the warrior who had taken his wife, he boiled like molten lava. The woman he loved, abducted. That Zach had just found out she was with child added to his rage. If anything happened to her, if anything happened to *them*, Zach would wage a war of extermination on the Bloods. He couldn't kill them all. They would probably slay him in the end. But he would rub out as many as he could. They would pay a hundredfold for what they had done.

Zach was so mad that when he had gone barely a hundred yards into the forest, he drew rein and took deep breaths to calm himself. He had to concentrate, to keep his senses sharp. The Blood would count on being pursued and be watching his back trail.

As McNair had pointed out, it was unlikely the warrior was alone. There must have been more. How many, Zach wouldn't know until he struck their trail. They were probably waiting in ambush. All the more reason for him to keep his wits and not let his wrath sweep him away.

The tracks were easy to follow, as fresh as they were. Zach came to where they entered a stream. He crossed to the other side and stopped. The ground was undisturbed. The warrior had stayed in the water and gone either upstream or downstream.

Zach reined around and rode to the middle. Bending as low as he could, he examined the stream bed. Much of it was gravel. Some of it was rock. Here and there was plain mud, and in a muddy spot a partial hoof pointed upstream toward the mountains to the west.

Straightening, Zach gigged the bay. He held his rifle across his saddle in front of him. Eyes narrowed, he scanned both banks. Sooner or later the warrior had to leave the stream, and when he did, there would be evidence of it.

Zach struggled to focus on the hunt. He kept thinking of Lou, of what she must be going through. It was like having a knife pierce his heart. The ache was almost more than he could bear.

He resisted the urge to fly blindly ahead so that he could rend the warrior limb from limb.

Zach would do it, too. When he caught up to them he would kill the warrior slow so that he suffered as few ever had. Anyone who would abduct a pregnant woman deserved no less.

Zach wondered how it was that the Bloods found the valley. There was only one way in, as far as he knew. His father and Shakespeare had blocked the other passes. They did it to keep something like this from happening, yet it had happened anyway. Life was fickle. The things a person least wanted to happen happened.

Zach remembered Lou's last embrace. How she had looked into his eyes, her own so happy and alive with love and the knowledge that in nine months they would be parents. She'd told him that she loved him. She said it a lot, far more than he did. His nose clogged and his throat grew tight. He went to cough to clear them but caught himself. Sounds could carry.

He wished his pa were there. There was no finer shot, no man alive more resourceful. With his pa at his side, Zach would be assured of rescuing Lou and bringing her home safe.

The grass on the left bank was trampled.

Zach drew rein. He had found where the Blood's horse climbed out. Of the Blood and Lou, there was no sign. Apparently the warrior had gone off up the mountain, perhaps to rejoin the rest of the war party. Zach poked the bay with his heels. The bay started out, slipped, and fell back when part of the bank broke and slid into the water.

The bay snorted and stamped.

"Easy, boy," Zach said, and patted its neck. He slapped his legs and the bay started up the bank a second time. It was even slipperier now, and loose dirt dribbled from under the bay's hooves.

"You can do it," Zach coaxed.

The bay lunged and dug in its rear hooves. It whinnied as if in pain. More of the bank broke off, but the bay made it up and over, and stopped.

Zach climbed down. He inspected each leg, and they appeared fine. "You seem all right to me." He went to climb back on and his gaze strayed to the ground ahead. Something pricked at him, a feeling that did not seem right somehow. It bore closer scrutiny.

Zach took a few steps. A downed pine branch was at his feet. He looked around. There were saplings on both sides, and grass and brush. All perfectly normal. Then he noticed another pine limb propped against a bent sapling, and he looked again at the pine limb at his feet, and it hit him that there wasn't a pine tree within fifty feet. The limbs couldn't have fallen there. They had to have been put there deliberately.

Zach edged around the limb. He saw a rope and two notched sticks rigged as a trigger. The bent sapling took on new significance. Careful not to bump the branch, he moved closer. At just the right height to impale a man on horseback was a sharp spike.

Zach grinned. It was a clever trap. No doubt there would be others. But they wouldn't stop him from rescuing Lou. The warrior who took her would come to rue the day.

Zach unlimbered his tomahawk. He had practiced throwing it so many times that hitting the two sticks was easy. The sapling whipped up, the spike cleaving thin air instead of him. Now any deer or elk that happened by wouldn't be hurt in his stead.

Picking up the tomahawk, Zach slid the handle under his belt. He climbed on the bay and raised the reins. "Nice try. But I'm coming for you, Blood. It's you or me, to the death."

The Outcast did not have a high opinion of white men. The few he had encountered had not impressed him. It was ridiculously easy to steal their horses. They made their campfires so big and so bright that the flames could be seen from far off. They made so much noise when they were on the move that they could be heard from far off, too. The whites were tough fighters, though. He would concede that much. Add to that the advantage their guns gave them, and it was wise not to take them lightly in battle.

The Outcast did not have a high opinion of half-breeds, either. Breeds were not as other men. The mixing of blood made them more violent than most. He had never seen this for himself, but he had heard it from so many people that it must be true. Breeds were also formidable fighters. Like whites, they should not be taken lightly.

The Outcast expected both the old white and the young breed to come after him. He had the female. She was perfect bait to draw them up into the mountains, where he could slay them.

So when the Outcast checked his back trail as he had done a hundred times that day and spotted a lone rider far below, he congratulated himself. The sapling with the spike must have gotten one of them. He tried to tell which one was still after him, the old man or the breed, but the distance was too great and he saw only the rider, who was in shadow, for a few brief moments.

No matter, the Outcast told himself. Whichever one it was, the rider was as good as dead. He continued to climb. His captive squirmed and looked up at him. She looked at him a lot and always in the same way. It bothered him. He turned his face away and pretended to be interested in a peak to the south.

Lou was weary and sore and scared. She was afraid that Zach or Shakespeare would be caught by the trap the warrior had set. She was worried, too, by pains in her belly, cramps that came and went. She didn't know if she could lose the baby so soon after she had conceived, but she did not want to take the risk. She wished her captor would stop and let her rest. She kept looking at him, but he ignored her.

The Outcast came out of the trees and drew rein at the base of a steep talus. To go up it would be foolhardy. The loose stones and dirt would give way. Many a mount had broken a leg on talus, which was why men who cared about their animals avoided them.

But the man who was after him, eager to save the female, might cast caution aside, especially if the Outcast gave him cause. With that in mind, the Outcast started up. He went only a short way, enough to suggest to his pursuer that he braved the slope and to get him to do the same. Then he reined to the right and rode in a loop that brought him down to the bottom.

It was not much of a trick. Anyone with keen

eyes would see that he had not gone all the way up. But he counted on his pursuer's worry for the woman making the man careless. It was worth trying, even if all it did was cripple the man's horse. An enemy afoot was easier to slay.

The Outcast circled the talus slope until he came to firm ground and turned up the mountain. The sun was bright on the rocky ramparts. High above, an eagle soared, its head white against the blue.

The Outcast liked this valley. It was abundant with life. It had occurred to him that if he killed the white men and the breed and whoever lived in the lodge at the east end of the lake, he would have the valley to himself. He liked that idea.

He had wandered far since being banished from his tribe. It wasn't that he wanted to, so much as he liked breathing. Lone warriors were inviting targets. That he had lasted so long spoke well of his prowess. But he was tired of always being on the move. It would be nice to have a place he could stay where others wouldn't bother him. It would be nice to have a lodge over his head once more.

Lou looked at him again. She needed rest. If he didn't stop soon, she would fling herself from the pinto, and the devil be damned. But just as she was girding herself, they reached the top of the talus and he reined along the upper edge a dozen yards and stopped. Raising a leg, he slid off, then reached up and lowered her to the ground. He wasn't gentle about it. She winced when a rock gouged her ribs. Rolling onto her side, she gazed down the slope.

Lou suspected he was up to something. The move he did at the bottom must be a ruse, but if it was, he was in for a surprise. Zach and

Shakespeare were too savvy to climb a talus slope. They would go around.

Lou struggled to sit up. Her wrists were chafed from the rope, and her ankles were sore. She hated the gag. She worried she might accidentally swallow it and choke. Glancing at her captor, she made noise and bobbed her head, trying to get him to look at her.

The Outcast was deep in thought. The trick alone might not be enough to get the rider out on the talus where he wanted him. An extra lure was called for. The sounds the woman was making gave him an idea. He put his hand on his knife, and she recoiled.

Lou thought he was going to stab her. She tensed, prepared to sell her life and the life inside of her as dearly as she could. He stepped around behind her and she went to pivot, when suddenly the strip of dress tied over her mouth fell away. He had cut it.

The Outcast came back around. He motioned for her to open her mouth wide. When she did, he carefully stuck two fingers in and pulled out the gag. He thought she might try to bite him, but she didn't.

Lou was so relieved, she smiled. She opened and closed her mouth, working her jaw muscles. Then she said, "I'm obliged." She knew he couldn't understand her but maybe he would take her meaning.

The Outcast grunted. He could tell she was grateful. It was silly of her to think he had done it to ease her discomfort. He wanted her able to make noise. He wanted her to help lure the rider onto the talus slope.

Lou tried talking to him in Shoshone. Zach had taught her enough to get by when they visited their village, which he liked to do at least two or three times a year. But it was plain the warrior didn't understand.

The Outcast wondered what tongue she was speaking. On an impulse he went behind her and untied her wrists but left her ankles bound.

Lou was delighted. She gingerly rubbed her chafed skin and said in English, "Thank you. That was kind of you."

His bow across his legs, the Outcast squatted where he could watch the slopes below.

An inspiration came over Lou. There *was* a way to communicate. She wasn't much good at it, but it was worth a try. She held her right hand up, palm out, her fingers well apart and pointed up, and wriggled her wrist several times. It was sign talk for 'question' or 'what.'

The Outcast gave a mild start. He didn't know that whites knew sign. His own people were adept at it.

Lou pointed at him. Then she held her right hand with her fingers closed and snapped her index finger at him. She had asked him what he was called. She figured that if she showed she was interested, he might be friendlier.

The Outcast was amused. Leave it to a female to ask his name when she should be begging him to spare her and her man. His fingers flowed swiftly in answer.

His reply puzzled Lou. She thought he said 'I am outside.' But that couldn't be right.

In the trees above, a jay took wing with loud shrieks.

The Outcast didn't see anything to account for it. He glanced down the mountain and stiffened. The rider was much closer. It was the breed, and he was coming fast, his gaze on the ground.

Lou looked in the same direction, and her breath caught in her throat. Zach was coming to save her!

It was working out exactly as the Outcast had planned. He slid an arrow from his quiver.

Chapter Eleven

Shakespeare McNair sat in the rocking chair in Zach and Lou's cabin. He didn't rock. He sat staring at the stone fireplace without seeing it. He was deep inside himself, adrift on tides of fear and despair.

Earlier he had carried Blue Water Woman into the bedroom and gently placed her on the bed. She was pale and sweaty, and never stirred. He felt her pulse and was appalled at how weak it was.

Shakespeare was worried worse than sick. He loved that woman, loved her with all that he was. She was his heart given form. He loved her so much that to see her like this tore him to his core. He felt as if his very being were being wrenched and twisted.

He had run out of tears. He had cried until there were none left. Now drained, he sat staring blankly into space and prayed that the woman who was everything to him would go on being everything to him. Life without her would be an unending emptiness.

Shakespeare had been in love twice in his life. Love of the marrying kind. His first wife had been kind and wonderful. After she died he lived alone for years until circumstance conspired to bring him back together with Blue Water Woman.

It was strange. Here Shakespeare thought he had loved his first wife with the deepest love anyone ever felt. But his love for Blue Water Woman eclipsed his first love as the sun eclipsed the earth. The depth of his devotion to her went beyond anything he ever knew. They had a pet expression—"hearts entwined"—that described better than any other words what they meant to each other.

Now she lay at death's door, and there was nothing Shakespeare could do but wait. Not that he had been idle. He never went anywhere without his possibles bag. In it were a fire steel and flint, a sewing needle, a whetstone, and other things he found regular use for. There were also various herbs.

To aid Blue Water Woman, first he applied a powder ground from the root of what the Shoshones called the wambona plant. It was the best of all medicines to stop bleeding.

Once Shakespeare was sure he had stopped it, he made a poultice from plantain and applied it with a cloth.

At moments like this, Shakespeare took issue with the Almighty. It seemed to him that the suffering people went through—and some folks went through a godawful lot of it—they were better off without. He wasn't one of those who thought life should be all cream and pie, but he was prone to wonder where the sense was in people hurting and dying.

Shakespeare roused and shook his head. Feeling sorry for himself wouldn't do any good. He rose and went into the bedroom. Blue Water Woman was as pale and still as before. He sat on the edge of the bed and placed his hand on her brow to see if she had a fever, and she opened her eyes.

"There you are."

Shakespeare nearly jumped. "You're awake!" He bent and kissed her right cheek and then her left, his eyes misting. "Damn, you gave me a scare."

Blue Water Woman licked her lips. She was unbearably weak, and her head throbbed. But she didn't dwell on the shape she was in. She saw the worry in his eyes and perceived the turmoil he was in, and did what she always did. She took his mind off his worries by asking, "Whose bed is this?"

"What?"

"A simple question. This is not ours. What kind of husband are you that you put me in a strange bed?"

"Now see here," Shakespeare said in some annoyance, "we're in Zach's cabin. He went off after the Blood who took Lou. I've done what I could for you and tucked you in."

"I want to be in our own bed."

"Later."

"I would like to go now."

"If you aren't the most contrary female who ever drew breath, I don't know who is. I'll take you to our cabin when you're up to it and not before."

"But—"

"Have you forgotten the knock on your noggin? Do you have any idea how much blood you've lost? It's best you lie here and get your strength back."

"Nate would take Winona if she asked him. Zach would take Lou."

"I never," Shakespeare said, and launched into a quote. " 'I will fetch you a toothpicker now from the furtherest inch of Asia. Bring you the length of Prestor John's foot. Fetch you a hair off the great Cham's beard. Do you any embassage to the Pygmies.' " He paused. "And whatever else your little heart desires."

Blue Water Woman mustered a wan smile.

"Share the humor, why don't you?"

"You are yourself again."

Emotion welled up in Shakespeare. Here she was, severely hurt, and she was more concerned about him. He tried to speak but couldn't for the constriction in his throat.

"Cat have your tongue?" said Blue Water Woman a white saying she remembered. "It must be some cat to stop yours from wagging."

Shakespeare looked away. He coughed, then carefully embraced her and whispered into her ear, "Have I told you lately how much I love you?"

"More than you love your mare?"

"A horse is a horse. You're mixing feathers and fur."

"More than you love your rifle?"

"Now you're just being silly. I'm fond of my gun, yes, because it keeps me alive. But I'd never ask it to marry me."

"More than you love the Bard?"

Shakespeare raised his head and looked at her. "Damn, woman. When you cut, you go for the jugular. But since you have put me on the spot, I'll confess." He stroked the soft sheen of her neck. "I love you more than I love old William S."

Blue Water Woman grinned. "At long last I know where I stand. I should be hit on the head more often."

Shakespeare laughed. She was acting more like her usual self every minute, and there was a pink blush to her cheeks that bode well for her recovery. "Is there anything I can get you? Anything at all?"

"How soon men forget. I want to be in my own bed."

"'Well moused, lion.' I will go make a travois."

"How sweet of you. And all I had to do was twist your arm."

Shakespeare McNair sighed.

Zach King was doing it again. He was being reckless. He knew it, but he couldn't stop himself. The sign was fresh. The tracks showed he was close to his quarry, close to the Blood who had taken the woman he loved, close to rescuing her. So he pushed hard up the slope, goading the bay when it flagged. He was so intent on the tracks that he came out of the forest and was a few feet up a talus slope when he realized what it was, and drew rein.

Zach raised his head. The tracks led onto the talus. He pursed his lips in puzzlement. Only a madman or a fool would try to cross talus. The Blood impressed him as neither. The spike on the sapling had been the work of a shrewd mind.

The ridge above the talus consisted of more

timber broken by large boulders. Nowhere was there any sign of Lou and her abductor. So they must have made it up.

Zach had a decision to make. Climb the talus, or be smart and safe and ride around it. Riding around would take longer. Since every second of delay was an eternity of suspense, he did what he knew he shouldn't. His father would have the good sense not to. The same with McNair. But Zach jabbed his heels against the bay and started up.

Almost immediately dirt and stones spilled from under the bay's heavy hooves. The bay snorted and stopped, and Zach urged it on again. He held his rifle low against his left leg, the reins in his right hand.

Up above, Lou was startled by a clatter. She looked down, and her heart leapt into her throat. It was Zach, coming to save her! She opened her mouth to shout a warning, and out of the corner of her eye, she saw the warrior smile.

The Outcast was pleased with himself. He had planned well. The woman would yell. The breed would forgo all caution and charge up the slope. The talus would bring the breed's horse down, leaving the breed on foot in the open, within range of his arrows. Then he realized the woman was looking at him.

A chill rippled through Lou. She knew that if she shouted, Zach would come flying up that treacherous slope—which she now suspected was exactly what her captor wanted him to do. She saw an arrow notched to his bowstring, an arrow meant to take her husband's life, and she acted out of sheer impulse, out of her love for the man who had claimed her heart. She threw herself at the warrior.

The Outcast was caught off-guard. He had expected the woman to shout. With her ankles bound, he'd felt she posed no threat. But suddenly she was on him, raking at his eyes with her nails, a fierce gleam in her eyes that made him think of a mountain lion protecting her kittens or a she-bear, her cubs.

Lou's one hope was to blind him. She couldn't hope to overpower him; he was much too big and too strong. So she clawed at his eyes with both hands while driving both her knees at his chest.

The Outcast was knocked back. He rolled as he hit the ground and she clung to him like a bobcat to its prey. He wanted to hold on to the bow, but if he did she would take out an eye.

Lou missed his eye but opened his cheek. He kept turning his head to thwart her. When he tried to roll on top of her, she kicked out with all her might with both legs.

The Outcast was sent tumbling. He lost the bow and the arrow and came to a stop on his stomach. Placing his hands flat, he went to push up and realized he was on the talus. He rose as high as his knees and looked up just as the white woman launched herself at him.

Lou gave no thought to her safety, no thought to the life in her womb. She thought only of Zach and what her captor would do to the man she loved if she didn't stop him. She slammed into the Outcast's chest so hard that it sent pain shooting from her shoulder to her hip. The next instant she was on her side and sliding.

The Outcast was sliding, too. He thrust his arm down to stop, but he was caught in a flowing current of stones and dirt.

Below, Zach drew rein in amazement at the sight of his wife and her warrior captor locked in mortal combat. He saw Lou hurl herself at the warrior and both of them tumble down the slope in a rush of broken earth. "Lou!" he bawled in alarm.

Louisa heard him. She sought to arrest her slide, but the stones tore at her palms and fingers. Her legs, bound as they were, were of little use. She remembered her father-in-law telling her once about the time he was caught in a talus slide, and how he had stayed limp and loose and let the talus sweep him along. So long as she didn't fight it, she might reach the bottom alive.

The Outcast dug in his heels and clutched at the talus, but he might as well have clutched at sand. He couldn't stop sliding. Worse, he was sliding ever faster and dislodging more and more. He was like a ball of snow sent rolling down, gathering speed and growing in size, and dirt covered him like a cloud, making him indistinct. It was hard to see.

Zach started to rein to Lou's aid and stiffened. A twenty-foot section of stone and earth was sweeping toward the bottom, carrying Lou and the Blood with it—and coming directly at him. He reined around, or tried to, and suddenly the bay was kicking and whinnying as the slope gave way under it. Zach threw himself clear as the bay came down on its side. Fortunately they hadn't climbed far. It was only a dozen feet to the bottom. Zach came to a stop and stood.

Lou swatted at the cloud of dust. She remembered her condition, and put her hands over her belly, fearing the outcome should she career into a boulder. She glimpsed Zach down at the bottom and was glad he was safe. Then she realized she was sliding toward him, along with tons of dirt and rock, and a warning cry was torn from her throat.

Zach looked up. He ran to the bay, grabbed the reins, and tugged. The horse pumped upright and stood trembling. Quickly, Zach swung on. He reined the bay around and sought to gallop out of there, but the next second the the talus was upon them. Stones and dirt and dust eddied about the bay like water. The horse managed a few strides and was brought down again, whinnying as they were swept toward the trees.

Once again Zach flung himself clear. A spruce loomed and he tried to roll to the right, but he only partially succeeded. His ribs exploded with agony, and he almost lost his grip on the Hawken.

Lou was on her back, her heels up, praying desperately for deliverance. She had lost sight of her husband. She could no longer see the warrior. Under her, the talus moved like a living thing, bearing her with it. She was helpless in its grip, an ant caught in an earthen cataract.

The Outcast was doing all he could to stop his fall, and everything he did failed. His hands were torn, his feet battered. The quiver was torn from his back. He twisted to try to get his arms and legs under him, and was sent toppling out of control. Vaguely, he was aware of a large boulder in his path. The thud of contact caused his senses to reel and the world to dim. He shook his head to clear

it in time to see another boulder. He hit it excruci-
atingly hard. He was conscious of flying through
the air, of slamming down, of being swept along, a
roar in his ears, dust in his nose and mouth and
eyes.

Zach turned to look for Lou. A fist-sized rock
shot at him like a cannonball and he went to duck,
but it caught him on the side of the head. He cart-
wheeled. The sky and the ground changed places.
A tree loomed. The world faded to black and he
felt dirt sliding over him, and then there was nothing, save an abyss that sucked him into its inky
depths.

Lou thought she would suffocate from all the
dust. It made her eyes sting and water. She blinked
and swiped at them with a sleeve and cleared them
in time to feel the dirt give way under her and her
body start to sink. Loose earth and stones flowed
over her. She swatted at it but there was too much
for her to stop it from covering her. She couldn't
help herself; she screamed.

As abruptly as it began, the slide was over. The
scream died and the roar faded and the rock-and-
dirt avalanche came to an end. In the ensuing silence, nothing moved.

The talus was empty of life.

Chapter Twelve

Indians used the travois when they moved from one site to another. It consisted of long poles lashed together and covered with a hide. Shakespeare McNair made sure the travois he rigged was good and sturdy before he covered it with a buffalo robe. Then he carefully carried his wife from the bed and out the front door. She was still much too weak, but she had recovered enough to put her arms around his neck and teasingly regard him with a playful gleam in her eyes.

"My, how strong you are. It is good to know the pots and pans will not strain you."

Shakespeare was turning so he could lay her gently down. "Pots and pans?"

"One of us must do the cooking and wash the dishes after we eat."

After wrapping her in the robe, Shakespeare stepped back. "There. You should be comfortable enough."

"Didn't you hear me?"

"Yes. I'm ignoring you. I wouldn't let you cook anyway, in the shape your in. Nor wash clothes nor knit nor fetch the eggs from the chicken coop. Leave it all to me."

"How kind you are," Blue Water Woman said merrily. "I had forgotten your domestic skills. You use them so rarely."

"'Dost thou jeer and flout me in the teeth?'" Shakespeare quoted.

"Not at all." Blue Water Woman smiled sweetly. "You would make some man a fine wife."

Shakespeare snorted in mock indignation. "'O curse of marriage, that we call these delicate creatures ours.'" He bent and kissed her on the cheek. "Don't think I don't know what you're up to, wench."

"Pardon me?"

"You're trying to keep me from worrying by taking my mind off that gash in your skull. But it won't work. I love you too much."

Blue Water Woman reached up and squeezed his hand. "As I love you, Carcajou."

Shakespeare closed the door. He came around the travois, climbed on the mare, and started off at a turtle's pace. "If I jostle you, I'm sorry. I'll do the best I can not to."

"You are most considerate." Blue Water Woman was warm and snug. She closed her eyes and felt the motion of the travois under her.

Despite his worry, Shakespeare was optimistic. It appeared she wasn't severely hurt. A couple of weeks to mend, and she would be her old self.

"Husband?"

"Yes, nag of my life?"

"How do you think Zach is faring?"

"That boy can handle himself better than most." But deep down Shakespeare was worried. Blood warriors were fierce fighters. He wished he could have gone with the boy.

"Husband?"

"Yes, oh chattering chipmunk?"

"Why do you think the Blood took Louisa?"

"Maybe he hankered for companionship." But Shakespeare doubted it.

The Blackfoot Confederacy was notorious for its hatred of whites. The last time he went to Bent's Fort he'd been surprised to hear that several priests had gone into Blackfoot country to convert them. It struck him about as silly as trying to get a griz to give up meat.

"Husband?"

"Will you hush and rest? You talk more now than before you got that knock on the noggin."

"I only wanted to say that after you get me home, you should go after Zachary."

"No."

"I will be fine by myself."

"It's still no."

"Zach and Lou might need you. I could not bear it if anything were to happen to them."

"I couldn't bear it if anything happened to you." The very thought made Shakespeare's eyes mist. "Zach will understand. He'd do the same if he were in my moccasins."

"May I ask you one more thing? And then I will be quiet."

Shakespeare shifted to check that the travois was dragging as it should. Sometimes the poles came apart if they weren't tied tight. "I'll believe that when I don't hear it. But go ahead. Ask away."

"Are you sure you would not like to have a child of our own? We could go to St. Louis and adopt."

"Are you insane? At our age?" Shakespeare

laughed. "My heart might say yes, but my aching joints say no. It's sweet of you, though."

They were halfway to Nate's cabin. The shore became rocky, so much so that Shakespeare reined closer to the trees, where the ground was largely rock free. He gazed at the wooded slopes to the west and spied a cloud of dust high up. The cloud grew, borne by the breeze. What caused it, he wasn't rightly sure.

"Husband?"

"So much for your promise. You are falser than vows made in wine."

"I insist you go find Zach and Lou. It will be partly my fault if they come to harm."

"How do you figure?"

"If I had not been hurt, you would have gone with him."

"Did you invite the Blood to our valley? Did you ask to be hit on the head? Quit being ridiculous." Shakespeare shifted in the saddle. "When I get you to our cabin, you had better still that tongue of yours or I will by god sew your mouth shut."

"You are adorable when you are angry."

Shakespeare had a retort on the tip of his tongue, but just then the undergrowth crackled and out of the forest lumbered the last thing he wanted to run into with his wife lying helpless on a travois and the mare unable to go any faster than a walk.

It was a bull buffalo.

The seven Tun-kua had seen the whole thing, and marveled at the destruction. They had crept to within an arrow's flight of the young white woman and the warrior and were watching from concealment. They saw the warrior cut her hands free and remove the gag.

When they used sign talk, Skin Shredder almost gave himself away. He rose higher to see better and the brush he was hidden in rustled. But neither the warrior nor the woman looked up. He didn't know which tribe the warrior belonged to. Since all tribes were his enemies, it didn't matter.

Skin Shredder was about to signal to begin the stalk when a rider appeared lower down. That it turned out to be the young breed was no surprise. His people knew that the breed and the young woman lived in the same lodge. The breed had come to save her.

Skin Shredder expected blood to be spilled. He decided to await the outcome. He was amazed when the white woman attacked the warrior. She had great courage, that one. He was even more amazed when they tumbled onto the talus and caused part of the slope to break away.

Now the sliding of the earth had ceased. The talus was still. Thick clouds of dust rose over it.

Skin Shredder slashed the air with a hand and he and his fellow warriors cautiously moved lower. The warrior's animal was tied to a tree and shied at their approach. Thanks to the breeze, the dust soon cleared—revealing nothing but talus.

"I do not see any of them," Splashes Blood declared.

"Nor I," Star Dancer said.

"We will circle around and search," Skin Shredder instructed "You three go that way. You others come with me."

"Do we finish them with arrows?" Star Dancer asked.

"It has been too long since our people ate a live heart. If they are breathing, we take them back with us."

To the Tun-kua, eating a heart was their most sacred ritual. Everyone took part. The sacrifice was fed a last meal the night before. At sunrise the sacrifice was stripped and washed and tied to a stake. Then came the dance of knives. By the time it was done the sacrifice was cut from head to toe. Usually they screamed and wailed. But they did not scream long. The taking of the heart came next; it was cut from them while they were alive. Then the medicine man would hold it aloft and go among them, and every Tun-kua—man, woman and child—would reverently touch it. The heart was then cut into small pieces, and a piece placed on the tongue of each.

More than any other ceremony, it spoke to who they were and firmed the bond they shared as Tun-kua.

Skin Shredder hoped they found one of the three alive.

Wisps of dust still rose. Here and there pebbles rattled.

They looked for bodies—an arm, a leg, anything.

"A bad way to die," Splashes Blood said.

"Not fit for a warrior," another agreed.

To Skin Shredder, death was death. His time would come one day, and he looked forward to it. The Tun-kua believed there were three spirit worlds in the afterlife: one for animals, another for enemies, and a third for Tun-kua. Life was much like it was in this world except there were no ailments or pain or misery, and the hearts tasted sweeter.

"They must be buried."

"Keep looking."

They were almost to the bottom when Star Dancer pointed. "There! It is the woman."

Skin Shredder saw her hand poking limply from the dirt and rocks. "She must be dead." No sooner did he say it than her fingers moved. "Link arms. We will form a chain. I will go out myself."

It was treacherous work. The talus could give way at any moment. But by taking small steps and treading lightly, they edged out until Skin Shredder was close enough to grip the woman's hand. Only a sprinkle of dirt covered part of her face and one shoulder.

Skin Shredder pulled. He had to do it in such a way that he didn't press down hard with his feet. Bit by bit, he dragged her from her earthen grave. Rocks rolled and the earth moved, but it didn't set the rest of the talus in motion.

The white woman groaned a few times. Her dress was torn and brown with dirt. Her face had many bruises.

Skin Shredder could not get over how hideous she was. She didn't have the broad nose or big lobes or thick eyebrows of Tun-kua women. She didn't have the tattoos that made Tun-kua women so beautiful. With infinite slowness, he stooped and picked her up. He was surprised at how light she was. He carefully handed her to Splashes Blood who in turn handed her to Star Dancer, who gave her to the last warrior in the chain; he set her on solid ground.

Once they were safe, they ringed the woman.

"Her ankles are still tied," Star Dancer noted.

Skin Shredder cut the rope. He shook her but all she did was groan. He shook her harder, and when that failed, he smacked her on the cheek. Her eyelids fluttered and then opened wide.

Lou could scarce credit what she saw. The last she remembered, she was hurtling down the talus slope. A wave of fright washed over her, but she didn't let it show. She knew about the tribe on the other side of the range. They called themselves the Heart Eaters and had those terrible faces. Her father-in-law and McNair had supposedly blocked the pass that permitted the Heart Eaters to enter King Valley, but apparently the warriors had found another way in.

From the frying pan to the fire, Lou realized. She smiled to show them she was friendly and slowly sat up. Her left shoulder throbbed and her face hurt all over. She looked around for Zach and fought down rising panic. "How do you do?"

Once again Skin Shredder was impressed by her courage. Most captives would cower in fright. "I do not speak your tongue."

Lou remembered Nate saying the Heart Eaters knew sign. She motioned at the talus and asked in finger talk, 'Question: You save me?'

'We pull you out.'

'I thank you.'

'We no do help you.'

'Question: What you want me?'

'We take you our village.'

Lou's breath caught in her throat. 'I no want go.'

'You go,' Skin Shredder signed with a cold smile.

Twisting, Lou searched the talus for Zach. He was nowhere in sight. He might be buried and likely dead. Her eyes started to tear, and she blinked them away. "Oh, Zachary."

Skin Shredder guessed she was looking for her man. He gestured, and Splashes Blood and Star Dancer seized her arms and hauled her to her feet. When they let go, she swayed like a reed and would have fallen if Star Dancer hadn't held her.

'Question: You hurt?'

'I be weak,' Lou responded. She could feel her strength slowly returning, but she didn't want them to know. The longer they delayed, the better her chance of spotting Zach, or what was left of him, and she dearly wanted to see him one last time, even if he lay in the repose of death.

To his friends Skin Shredder said, "We will wait, unless one of you wants to carry her."

No one did.

'Question,' Lou signed. 'What you do with me in village?'

Skin Shredder held his hand close to his chest, his fingers hooked like claws. He pretended to claw his chest open and pull his heart out. Then he held his hand up to his mouth and pretended to take a bite.

The other warriors laughed.

Louisa King shuddered.

Chapter Thirteen

A small herd of mountain buffalo called King Valley home. Shaggier than their flatland cousins, they stayed deep in the woods most of each day, coming out at dawn and late afternoon to drink and graze. They posed no threat so long as they were not disturbed. Many a time Shakespeare had watched them from his window and been reminded of the days when he hunted their cousins with his Indian friends. He didn't hunt these. Nate had suggested they leave the herd be. As Nate put it, "We'll hunt them only if we're starving. That way, we'll always have a pantry on the hoof we can fall back on."

Shakespeare got a chuckle out of *pantry on the hoof.*

But now, with his wife helpless on the travois, Shakespeare worried their decision would cost him dearly.

The bull snorted and shook its shaggy head, its horns glinting in the sunlight.

Blue Water Woman heard the snort and craned her neck to see over the top of the travois. A tongue of fear licked at her and she swallowed it down. As she always did in a crisis, she willed herself to stay calm, to focus and not give sway to fright. "Husband?" she said softly.

Shakespeare didn't take his eyes off the buffalo. He was holding his Hawken across his legs, but he made no attempt to raise it. "Not now, chipmunk. We have a problem."

"I see him. You should cut the travois loose and ride off before he charges."

Shakespeare almost gave a snort of his own. "And abandon you? That's the silliest thing you've ever said in all the years I've known you."

The bull stamped and tossed its head and came several steps nearer. Over six feet high at the shoulders, with a bulging hump and broad head, it was a living, breathing monster.

Shakespeare fingered his rifle. It would take a lucky shot to bring the brute down. It must weigh between fifteen hundred and two thousand pounds, a lot of it muscle.

Blue Water Woman rose on an elbow. The bull looked at her and rumbled in its chest.

"For God's sake, don't move," Shakespeare cautioned. "If it charges I might not be able to protect you."

"If it charges I want you to save yourself."

Shakespeare did what he had just told her not to do; he moved. Turning in the saddle, he declared, "I can hardly forbear hurling things at you."

"I cannot help it if I love you and do not want you hurt."

"Grant me the same courtesy." Shakespeare had never told her, but he secretly hoped he died before she did. He would be so lonely without her, he didn't know if he would want to go on living.

Blue Water Woman was watching the buffalo. She was taken aback when other dark shapes appeared. Six, seven, eight, she counted, all as shaggy but none as big as the huge bull. "Carcajou!"

Shakespeare's pulse quickened. One buffalo was bad enough. Nine was a nightmare. All those horns, on creatures as unpredictable as the weather. He eased the Hawken from his lap. He couldn't get all of them, but he would bring the big bull down.

"Do not shoot," Blue Water Woman cautioned. She worried that he might drop the bull in the hope the rest would run off.

"What do you take me for?" Shakespeare wedged the hardwood stock to his shoulder and took aim.

"What are you doing then?"

"Just in case." Shakespeare intended to fire and throw himself in front of the travois, if it came to that.

"You are not to shoot no matter what," Blue Water Woman insisted. She was all too aware of how stubborn he could be once he set his mind to something.

"That will be for me to decide."

A cow started toward them, but stopped at a bellow from the bull.

"That was nice of him," Blue Water Woman said. Her gratitude was short-lived.

Head bobbing, blowing noisily, its hooves ringing on rocks, the big bull advanced.

Shakespeare took a bead on the buffalo's right eye. The skull was so thick that a brain shot rarely penetrated, and facing it head-on, he didn't have a lung shot. His best bet was the eye, but with the head bobbing as it was, it was like hitting a bobbing dark pea.

Blue Water Woman gripped the travois. She had seen for herself how savage buffalo could be when they were provoked. Once, after a surround, she had gone with the other women to skin and carve the many buffalo the warriors killed. She had been slicing a belly open when she heard cries and shouts. A bull everyone thought was dead wasn't. It had regained its feet, and before any of the warriors could loose more shafts, it had been among them, ramming with its broad forehead and ripping with its great horns. Four horses had gone down, one with its insides spilling out. A warrior had rode up and buried a lance in the buffalo's side, and the buffalo whirled and gored his horse. As the horse fell, the man was pitched onto an upcurved horn. For as long as she lived, Blue Water Woman would never forget his death shriek.

Shakespeare's impulse was to fire before the bull reached them. His finger curled around the trigger.

"Please, Carcajou."

Against his better judgment, Shakespeare took his cheek from the Hawken. His nerves jangled as the bull came ever closer. The mare nickered and tried to shy but couldn't because of the travois. "There, there," he said quietly, and stroked the mare's neck.

Blue Water Woman held her breath.

A swarm of flies buzzing around it, the big bull reached the mare. It looked at her, grunted, and walked on by.

Now it was beside the travois. Blue Water

Woman could have reached out and touched it. She saw its nostrils flare, and suddenly it stopped. The great head swung toward her. For a few heartbeats she feared the worst. The bull sniffed the buffalo robe she was bundled in, then nuzzled it and rubbed against the travois so hard that the entire travois shook and threatened to shatter.

Shakespeare put his cheek to the rifle.

The bull ambled on. After it came the bull's harem, none of them so much as giving the mare or the travois a glance. They crossed to the lake and dipped their muzzles to drink.

"I'll be switched," Shakespeare said in relief, and gigged the mare to get out of there.

Blue Water Woman sank onto her back. Tension drained like water from a sieve. "Are you glad you listened to me?"

"I always listen to you, heart of my heart."

"Oh my," Blue Water Woman said.

"What?"

"All this time I thought you were deaf."

A ringing in Zach's ears was his first sensation. He clawed up out of a dark well and floated in a pool of pain. Where he was and why he was in pain eluded him until he tried to move and discovered his arms and legs were pinned. Then it all came back in a rush: the talus, Lou, the Blood warrior, everything. He opened his eyes and brown specks fell into them, making them water. Blinking, he raised his head. He was on his back. Dirt and rocks formed a cocoon around him. Only his face was exposed.

That he was alive was a quirk of fate. If he had wound up facedown, he'd have suffocated. He thought of Lou—and sought to break free. Dust got into his nose, making him cough. He cut his fingers, but he didn't care. After hard effort he was able to sit up. He looked around. The talus had swept him into the pines.

A lot of tugging and digging freed his legs. He slowly rose, half dreading a leg was broken. He was bruised and sore but otherwise fine

His rifle was missing. He'd also lost one of his pistols. A glint of metal drew him to the Hawken's barrel, which poked from a bush. He picked it up and was relieved to find it undamaged except for scrapes and nicks. He looked around again but did not see the pistol.

Zach moved out of the pines. The talus slope was much as it had been. He scoured it from bottom to top, but there was no sign of Louisa. He cupped his mouth to shout her name and hesitated. If the Blood was alive, the warrior would hear and come after him. Zach shouted anyway.

The silence was a stab to his gut.

Zach moved along the edge of the talus, seeking some sign. A whinny brought more relief as the bay came out of the trees. It was covered with dust and the parfleche he had tied on was missing, but otherwise the horse was unhurt. He climbed on and called Lou's name again.

Worry clawed his insides. He imagined her buried alive. It would be an awful way to go. He debated whether to scale the slope on foot and search every square inch. Instead he swung wide and rode to the top. Dismounting, he checked for sign. In the dirt were tracks—a lot of tracks. They told a story that sent a thrill of joy and then a chill of horror down his spine.

Lou was alive! But other warriors had her. Her footprints led to where a horse had been tied. From there, hoofprints led up the mountain, with the tracks of warriors on either side.

Zach knew of the tribe on the other side of the divide; he had fought and killed one of its warriors. His pa and Shakespeare had used a keg of black powder to blow the pass—the only way over, they thought. Apparently there was another, and a war party had come into the valley. Those warriors now had Lou and were taking her back to their village.

That was how Zach read the sign. Lou faced a worse end than if she had been entombed in the talus.

Zach swallowed and gigged the bay. He figured they weren't far ahead, no more than an hour, but they would move fast and it would take some doing to overtake them before they got over the range.

A grim fury seized him. All Zach wanted was to live in peace with his wife and the others. All he asked was to be left alone by the outside world. His days of living to count coup were over. But enemies kept putting them in peril. Danger kept rearing its unwanted head. Life was a constant struggle for survival, and he was tired of it.

The idea surprised him. He had never thought like this before. And now was hardly the time to start.

The Heart Eaters had his wife.

So be it.

He would have to save her and take their lives, or perish in the attempt.

From the woods below the talus, the Outcast watched the breed head up the mountain. Limping into the open, he started after him. His left knee throbbed and his head pounded. He'd lost his bow and his quiver, but he still had his knife and tomahawk. They would have to do.

The Outcast had not lost consciousness. For a while he had lain in a daze but finally he recovered enough to stand on wobbly legs. He almost gave himself away when he had moved through the trees, but fortunately he saw the seven warriors before they saw him.

They were strange, these warriors. The Outcast had never beheld their like. Their scarred faces were hideous. He imagined they did it to strike fear into their enemies, but he could have been wrong. He saw them uncover the white woman, saw their hand talk although they were too far away for him to tell what they were signing. Then the warrior had made the woman climb onto his pinto and they went off up the mountain.

The Outcast had two reasons to go after them— they had taken his horse and his captive. A third reason gnawed at him like a beaver at a tree, but he refused to let it take root. He cared for no one but himself. He had lost all feelings for others the day *she* died.

Or, rather, the day he killed her and their baby.

He relived it in his mind, that terrible event, seared into his memory forever. The day he came back to his lodge to find Mad Wolf there. She had the baby to her bosom and was pleading with Mad Wolf to leave.

For half a dozen moons Mad Wolf tried to win her away. Mad Wolf had more horses and his father was high in the council, and he thought he had the right to any woman he wanted. Mad Wolf wanted Yellow Fox. Mad Wolf didn't care that she was spoken for. Mad Wolf didn't care that she had told him over and over that she would never come to live with him.

Mad Wolf kept after her. One fateful day he had dared to enter their lodge and press his suit.

The Outcast had never been so mad. Even now, it made his blood grow hot in his veins. They had heated words, Mad Wolf and he. One angry word led to another, and Mad Wolf reached for his knife.

Without thinking, the Outcast reacted. He drove his lance into Mad Wolf's body with all the strength in his sinews.

The Outcast hadn't realized that Yellow Fox had come up behind Mad Wolf. He hadn't realized his lance went all the way through Mad Wolf and through the baby and into her until she cried out.

It wasn't one body that fell.

It was three.

It was the day the Outcast died inside. When the elders called him before them, he listened with an empty heart. No Kainai had ever done such a thing. Kainai were never to kill Kainai. To kill a woman and an infant—it was unthinkable. It was bad medicine. With deep regret the council acted for the good of all.

They banished him.

No one came to see him off the day he rode from the village. Those he passed turned their backs to him.

The Outcast wandered. An empty vessel that refused to be filled, he traveled where whim took him. In his sorrow and grief he thought he would never feel again.

He hadn't, until now.

In grim anger, the Outcast started after the scarred warriors.

They had taken his horse and his captive.

He would have their lives—or they would have his.

Chapter Fourteen

"There." Star Dancer pointed.

"I see him," Skin Shredder said.

The breed was after them. As yet he was well down the mountain, but climbing rapidly.

"He will overtake us before the sun goes down."

"Let him." Skin Shredder would rise high in the esteem of his people if he brought back two captives instead of one.

Louisa wondered what they were talking about. She was on the pinto a little way ahead in the trees and could not see where they were looking. She hoped against hope that Zach was coming. She refused to believe he was dead. She'd survived the talus; so could he. He was a lot tougher.

The Heart Eaters continued their ascent.

Lou was tempted to try to escape. All she had to do was yank the reins from the hands of the Indian holding them, and use her heels. But with warriors on both sides and the leader and his friends behind, she would be lucky if she got ten feet.

Lou had to do something. Not just for her sake. She had the new life to think of. If something had happened to Zach, she owed it to him to stay alive so she could give birth to his legacy.

Lou put a hand on her belly. It was too soon to feel the baby kick, but she told herself that now and then she felt it move. Her imagination, most likely, but there it was.

Skin Shredder was watching her. He'd noticed how she was constantly putting a hand on her stomach. At first he thought she had been hurt when she was caught in the talus. Then he thought maybe she was sick. Finally he remembered his own women and the one who had just given him a son, and he blurted, "She is with child."

Splashes Blood looked at him. "Who?"

"How many captives do we have?" Skin Shredder nodded at the white woman. "We must keep her alive until it is born." Of all the delicacies life offered, of all the delicious kinds of meat, the heart of a baby was the choicest.

"The other Bear People will come after us," Splashes Blood mentioned.

Skin Shredder knew of whom he spoke—the giant with the black beard and the old man with the white beard. They were dangerous, that pair. "Let them come to our valley. They will never leave it."

A slope of lodgepole pines was mired in gloom. The slender trees grew in ranks so close together that at times there was barely space for the pinto. Skin Shredder doubted the white woman would try to escape until they were out of them. She could not ride fast with the trees pressing in on her. He relaxed his guard and stopped watching her.

Lou was bubbling with excitement. Here was her chance. She girded herself, and when most of the warriors were looking the other way, she coiled her legs and leaped. Her outstretched hands wrapped around a lodgepole, and with a lithe swing she was on the ground and running. She moved so quickly that she had a five-yard lead before a harsh cry alerted her captors to her flight.

Lou was fleet of foot. She wasn't as fast as Zach, but he often liked to say that she was a female antelope. In britches, anyway. Dresses slowed her. She poured all she had into her legs and bounded down the mountain in long loping strides. She risked a glance over her shoulder and saw that four of the Heart Eaters were after her. The rest had stayed with the pinto.

Skin Shredder was startled by how fast she was. He was going all out, but he couldn't gain. Star Dancer, though, was faster, and would catch her before she was out of the lodgepoles.

Heavy breathing and the thud of flying feet warned Lou one of them was almost on top of her. She dared another glance and saw bronzed fingers reaching for the back of her dress. The warrior was intent on her to the exclusion of all else. Inspiration struck, and she ran straight at one of the pines. The warrior's fingertips brushed her, and he smiled, thinking that he almost had her. He didn't see the tree until Lou swerved.

Skin Shredder heard the thud of impact. He didn't stop. He streaked past Star Dancer, who was holding an arm and thrashing about in pain. Now it was up to him.

Lou was pleased with herself. Her little ploy had worked. But now their leader was hard after her, and she didn't think the same trick would work twice. She started weaving among the slender boles, turning right and left, never running straight for more than a few yards. As she hoped, he lost a little ground.

Skin Shredder fumed. She was clever, this white woman. He settled into a rhythm, pacing himself, conserving his energy for a spurt when his chance came to catch her. And it would. He could run for many leagues without tiring. His stamina was superior to hers, and in the end, it would be her undoing.

An ache in Lou's side reminded her of how long it had been since she had run any distance. Cabin life had softened her. Add to that her condition, and it was small wonder that soon she was panting and her legs pained in protest at their abuse.

Lou refused to stop. She would never give up, not so long as she had breath in her body. She weaved right, ducked under a limb, weaved left and had her cheek opened. A branch snatched her dress and broke.

Skin Shredder admired her tenacity. She was so slight and frail that he would not have thought she had it in her.

The lodgepoles were almost at an end. Below was a slope sprinkled with spruce.

Lou must do something to slow Skin Shredder, but what? The breaking of the limb gave her an idea. She deliberately ran at another and snapped it off without breaking stride. Then, twisting, she threw the branch at his face.

Skin Shredder was caught by surprise. It was so unexpected, and she was so quick, that he swerved aside a fraction too late. The branch slashed his temple, missing his eye by a finger's width. He slowed, and she increased her lead.

Skin Shredder smiled. She was a firebrand, this small one. It was too bad she must die. She had the kind of spirit he liked in his wives.

Lou was glad she had slowed him down but she was only delaying the inevitable. She would run out of tricks and energy and the warriors would be on her. She imagined they would be mad, imagined them hitting and kicking her. A beating might cost her the baby. Added incentive for her to make her feet fly.

Lou was running so fast, the trees were a blur. She burst from the lodgepoles. A boulder filled her vision and she swept around it. On the other side was a badger mound and a badger hole. She willed her body to jump but she was not quite quick enough.

Her left foot went into the hole, and down she crashed.

Zach King pushed the bay harder than he had ever ridden it. He lashed the reins and used his heels and climbed as fast as the terrain permitted. The steep slopes chafed at his patience. His temper, held in check by a thin veneer of self-control, snapped. The more he thought about what Lou had gone through—first abducted by the Blood and now the Heart Eaters—the angrier he became.

Zach was in the grip of bloodlust. It made him think of when he was younger, when he lived for counting coup. He hadn't felt this way in many a moon, and it felt good to be his old self again.

He was eager for a glimpse of Lou and her captors. He had checked the Hawken and his remaining pistol. His knife was razor sharp. His tomahawk had a keen edge. He craved the coming fight as a drunk craved a drink or a person with a sweet tooth craved pies and cakes.

Whenever he came to a gap in the trees Zach rose in the stirrups and scanned the higher slopes. He figured the Heart Eaters were making for their secret pass over the top of the range. After he dealt with them and got Lou safely back home, he would take a keg of black powder and ensure the Heart Eaters never again invaded King Valley.

Better yet, Zach would like to find their village. Two or three kegs should suffice to blow the tribe to the white man's kingdom come—or enough of them that the few left would retreat deeper into the mountains and cease to be a threat to his loved ones or anyone else.

That had been one of life's hardest lessons. His father and mother were such good people, and they had raised him with so much kindness and love, that when he was little he took it for granted that everyone else was the same. It had come as a shock to discover that a lot of people weren't kind or loving—that they were, in fact, anything but. A lot of folks didn't care about anything except themselves. Even worse, some people, red and white, lived to hurt others. They relished the pain they inflicted, whether physical or emotional. They were hateful and mean, and reveled in their vileness. His pa said it was the way of the world. He thought they should all be chucked off a cliff.

Zach rose in the stirrups. He saw no one and was about to sink back down when he caught movement near a phalanx of lodgepole pines. It took a few seconds for what he was seeing to make sense. When it did, his breath caught in his throat. Lou was on foot and fleeing for her life.

He reached for his parfleche to take out his spyglass and remembered he had left it on a shelf in their bedroom.

"Damn my stupidity, anyhow."

Lou suddenly stumbled—or so it appeared to Zach—and fell. The others were on her in a twinkling. One of them yanked her to her feet and hauled her toward the lodgepoles. The others bent and seemed to be carrying or rolling something up the slope.

Zach raised the Hawken to his shoulder but lowered it again. What was he thinking? They were too far off. He must keep his temper in check for a little while longer.

He hoped Lou was all right, hoped the fall hadn't hurt her inside. If she should lose the baby he would wreak bloodshed on the Heart Eaters a hundredfold.

God, how Zach wished the bay had wings. Presently he neared the lodgepoles and reined toward the spot where he had seen Lou fall. He saw a badger burrow and guessed the truth. He also saw a bare shallow circle of dirt, and then another, each about as big around as a washtub. Ruts led from the circles into the trees. He wondered what made them.

A loud snapping and crunching brought Zach to a stop. He looked up just as a boulder came rolling out of the trees—straight at him. He reined sharply aside, fearing the boulder would crash into the bay's legs and bring down the horse. It missed by an arm's length.

Then Zach understood. The circles of dirt were where boulders had been. He reined to the left to get out of there just as another boulder hurtled out at the bay.

The horse carried them clear.

Zach went to rein around. Suddenly scarred figures burst from cover and swarmed about him. For a moment he thought he would be riddled with arrows, but their bows were slung. They had large rocks and tree limbs, and one let fly with a rock that struck the Hawken and nearly knocked it from his hand. He tried to point it, but the blunt end of a thick limb caught him in the ribs and iron fingers grabbed hold of his leg.

Zach was unhorsed. He slammed to the earth on his shoulders. Before he could rise, before he could draw his knife or his tomahawk, they were on him. A warrior was on each arm, a warrior on each leg, another astride his chest. He was pinned flat.

Zach heaved upward, but their combined weight was too much. They made no attempt to stab him or beat him. All they did was hold him down and smile. Those smiles were like searing red-hot pokers driven into Zach's gut. He felt a berserker rage coming over him, but he held it in check. All he would do was waste himself.

Two more warriors appeared, Lou held between them. She was limping, her face etched in pain. She smiled, a smile of such love and tenderness that Zach's head swam.

"About time you showed up."

Caught in an ebb tide of emotion, Zach said quietly, "I sure made a mess of it."

Louisa yearned to go to him and take him in her arms. She had tried to shout a warning, but

Skin Shredder had clamped a hand over her mouth. "We're not dead yet."

"How bad is your leg?"

"It's not broken." Lou gazed down the mountain. "Are you alone?"

"Shakespeare is tending Blue Water Woman."

"She's alive?"

"Yes."

"Thank God."

"Don't give up hope. I'll get you out of this or die."

"Haven't you heard?" Lou smiled. "I'm a King. A King never gives up hope."

Skin Shredder was puzzled. He couldn't understand how the two could be so calm about the breed's capture. He'd expected the man to be in a frenzy and the woman to scream and fight. Instead they behaved as if it were of no consequence. "Tie his wrists and bring his horse. Do not let him get on it. Make him walk."

Zach resisted when they hauled him to his feet and forced his arms behind him, but there were too many. It was humiliating, being bound by enemies.

They started up the mountain.

Lou walked beside Zach, her shoulder brushing his. None of the warriors objected until she made bold to reach out and gently clasp his bounds hands. The warrior behind her, evidently thinking she was trying to undo the knots, swatted her hands and said something.

Skin Shredder was in the lead. He glanced back when he heard Star Dancer tell the white woman not to touch the breed. "Watch her closely. They must not escape." It had been many moons since a raiding party brought back two captives. His people would be overjoyed. They would sing his praises and dance and cut out and eat the man's heart. The woman could wait until the baby was born. Then there would be two more to eat.

The thought made his mouth water. He could almost taste them.

Chapter Fifteen

Zach King trudged gloomily along, his thoughts as dark and ominous as a thunderhead. He had failed his wife, failed the one he loved. He had let himself be caught, and now their fate and the fate of their unborn child were in the hands of warriors with no mercy in their souls.

Not that Zach would give up. Lou had been right about being a King. Among the many lessons he learned from his parents was the most important: Never, ever give up or give in. No matter what life threw at him, no matter the challenge, no matter the peril, never surrender.

So as Zach trudged, he pondered. He must get Lou out of there. On horseback would be best, but if not then on foot. He must do it before they passed over the divide, while they were still in King Valley.

The Heart Eaters had taken his weapons. But they couldn't take his mind, and the mind was the most useful weapon of all. A mind could scheme. A mind could plot. A mind could come up with a way to snatch life from the fangs of death. A mind could defy fate.

Zach studied his captors without being obvious. With him bound, they must figure he wasn't much of a threat. None had arrows nocked to their bows. Only one kept a hand on the hilt of his knife. The others seemed to take it for granted that he would not give them trouble, not with his wife in their clutches.

Little did they realize that was all the more incentive for Zach to slay them. But Lou presented a problem. She had hurt her leg and limped with every step. She couldn't run fast or far. So whatever he came up with must take her handicap into account.

Zach glanced at her and saw she was smiling at him. "What?"

"I am happy you are here." Lou was near giddy with glee, in fact. She thought she had lost him in the slide.

"You're happy they caught me?"

"No, silly." Lou laughed. "I'm happy you weren't killed."

"If they have their way, we will be."

Lou stared at the warriors on either side. "We've been in tight situations before, but this is one of the worst."

"I'll get you out of this or die trying."

Lou touched his arm. "I'd rather you didn't. I'm going to have a baby and she'll need a pa."

"There you go again."

Lou hoped for a girl. Zach wanted a boy. The next nine months promised to be one long argument because neither—Lou caught herself. Here she was, thinking of their future, when it was very much in doubt they would live out the week.

Zach squinted skyward. They had several hours of daylight left. More than enough. The question was, when? He must pick the right time and place.

Louisa said quietly, "I want to tell you now, in case I don't get the chance later, how much I love you. How much having you as my husband has meant to me. How proud I have been to be your wife."

"You sound like you're saying good-bye."

"It's just that there are things that need to be said and this might be my only chance."

"I won't let them harm you."

"I know you'll do your best. You always do. You're as fine a man as any woman could ask for."

Zach shook his head. "I'm a hothead. I don't have much patience. I don't always consider your feelings. I tend to do what I want when I want and the rest of the world be damned."

Louisa grinned. "I didn't say you don't have flaws. Everyone does. But as flaws go, yours I can live with. You more than make up for them by being a devoted husband."

"I don't do any different than my pa."

"That's just it," Lou said. "Your pa had always put your ma and you and your sister before everyone and everything else. A lot of men don't do that. They'd rather drink and carry on with their friends than spend time with their families."

Zach was puzzled by why she was talking about how they got along at a time like this. There were more important things, such as how they were going to escape.

"They're not stopping us," Lou said.

"What?"

"They're letting us talk. I was testing to see if they would, or if they would make us stop." Lou stepped on a pine cone and her foot slipped, sending a sharp pain up her hurt leg.

Zach noticed. "Is it getting worse?"

"I can manage."

Zach had his doubts. She could barely walk. What would she do when they had to run for their lives? "I want you to stick close to me from here on out."

"You and only you."

The next slope was thickly forested. High above were sheer cliffs. A game trail bought them slowly and sinuously higher, until they came out on a short grassy bench. From there they could see for miles.

Lou paused to admire the view. She could see the lake and the brown square that was their cabin. She would give anything to be back there now, rocking in her chair or cooking, or maybe taking a stroll along the shore. She loved that more than just about anything.

The warrior behind her pushed her.

Lou stumbled. She tried to recover her balance, but her bad leg flared and she grabbed at Zach to keep from falling.

The warrior cuffed her.

So unexpected was the attack that Zach was rooted in rage for all of five seconds. Then he exploded. Whirling, he kicked the man in the leg. The warrior doubled over and Zach kneed him in the face. He drew back his foot to kick again, but a blow to his back sent him tottering toward the edge of the shelf. His heel came down on slick grass, and the next Zach knew, he was tumbling out of control. For harrowing moments he thought he would slam into a tree, but he came to a stop unhurt.

Two Heart Eaters were coming after him.

Heaving upright, Zach ran. It took some doing with his hands bound behind him. Angry shouts followed, and the crackle of underbrush. He rounded a boulder and nearly collided with a large log. Vaulting over, he dropped onto his side and pressed against it.

Feet padded. A warrior flew around the end. The second man leaped over the log as Zach had done—and over Zach, as well. Both raced on down the slope, unaware they had gone past him.

Scrambling erect, Zach stayed low and paralleled the bottom of the bench. He ran until he was out of sight of the warriors up above. Casting about, he searched for a flat rock with a serrated edge. He'd about despaired of finding what he needed when a godsend appeared at his feet. He set to sawing at the rope.

Angry yells told him more Heart Eaters had joined the search. From the sound of things only a few were guarding Lou.

Zach sawed and sawed. A few strands parted. Back and forth, back and forth, until his wrists and fingers ached. The rock was no knife. At the rate he was cutting it would take minutes he didn't have. He pressed harder. The rock bit into his palm, but pain was the least of his worries.

Below, the Heart Eaters went on hunting him. They had gone quiet, save for an occasional yell.

Zach felt blood on his palm. He kept cutting. More strands were severed. Impatient to rescue Lou, he stopped slicing, bunched his shoulders and tensed his arm muscles and exerted all his strength. He wasn't as immensely strong as his pa, but he was solid muscle. His body protested, but he strained and strained until, with an audible snap, the rope broke.

Quickly, Zach climbed to the top of the bench. He peered over. Forty feet away stood Lou, staring down the facing slope, her pretty face mirroring concern. Two warriors had been left to guard her. Beyond were the bay and the pinto.

Zach debated. Forty feet was a lot of open space. Both warriors had arrows notched to the strings of their bows. He couldn't possibly reach them before one or both of those shafts transfixed his body.

The warriors were talking.

Zach hefted the rock he had used to cut the rope. Then, cocking his arm, he threw it as high and as far as he could toward the other end of the shelf. Luck favored him and it came down in a tree, clattering from branch to branch as it fell. Both warriors whirled. Raising their bows, they moved toward the tree.

Zach exploded up over the bench and sprinted toward Lou and the horses. He remembered that one of the Heart Eaters had put his pistol, tomahawk, and knife in the parfleche on the bay.

Lou heard him and spun. She beamed in relief, only to have her husband fly past her. He was so intent on the bay that he didn't see what she saw—one of the warriors had gone into the trees, but the other had turned and was sighting down a barbed shaft. Lou went to cry a warning.

Zach had to pass the pinto to reach the bay. He was almost to it when the pinto whinnied and stepped directly into his path. He thought he was the cause until it wheeled and he saw blood welling from a long cut on its flank. In its flight it collided with the bay, and both horses bolted toward a warrior reaching for another shaft in his quiver.

The man leaped aside to avoid being trampled. He did not quite have the arrow out when Zach launched himself like a cannonball. His shoulder caught the warrior full across the chest. Down they went with Zach on top. Both grabbed for the hilt of the knife the warrior wore. Zach got his hand on it, but the warrior clamped hold of his wrist.

Zach punched him, a jab to the jaw that rocked the warrior's head. The man didn't let go. A second punch did no good, either, so Zach drove his forehead into the man's face. There was a *crunch* and moist drops spattered Zach's brow. But still the man held on to Zach's wrist.

Zach hit him in the throat and the warrior broke into convulsions. He raised his fist for a last blow, only to have small hands seize his forearm.

"Forget him!" Lou urged. "We must flee."

Shouts from below warned Zach why. The horses had made such a racket in running off that Skin Shredder and the others were hurrying back. Snatching the knife, he grabbed her hand and headed up the mountain.

Lou grit her teeth and did her best to keep up. She couldn't stop limping, though, and they went only a short way when before Zach slipped an arm around her and practically began carrying her.

"I can manage on my own."

"Hush and run."

The last thing Lou wanted was to slow him down. She pumped her good leg and put as little weight on her bad as she could. For a while that helped. They went more than fifty yards, into growth so thick the Heart Eaters would have to be right on top of them to see them. She began to think that maybe, just maybe, they would get away.

Zach was listening to the sounds of pursuit. Four or five warriors were spread out in a line.

Lou hurt worse with every step. She clung tight to Zach, furious at herself, yet elated they were eluding their pursuers. Or were they?

Zach sought a place to hide. A cave, a crevice, anything, so long as it would shelter Lou while he led the Heart Eaters away. He would gladly sacrifice himself for her sake and the sake of the baby.

Lou looked back. A swarthy, scarred form was plowing through the vegetation. Any moment he might spot them. She pulled on Zach, whispering urgently, "We need to find cover! Now!"

Zach did as she wanted. He didn't ask why. He darted into some aspens and threw himself to the ground, pulling her after him.

Lou's heart hammered. When the warrior flew past, she breathed a little easier.

Zach didn't linger. Helping her up, he bore to the north. He hoped the change of direction would confuse the Heart Eaters.

The woods became ominously still. The wind died, and not so much as a pine needle moved.

Zach liked it better when he could hear their pursuers. He slowed so they weren't making as much noise.

Lou accidentally put all her weight on her hurt leg. Torment racked her. She clamped her mouth shut to keep from crying out and was grateful when Zach stopped and hunkered. She squatted beside him, her hands on the ground for support.

"I think we lost them," Zach whispered. Now all they had to do was make it down the mountain to their cabin.

"I've hardly ever been so scared," Lou confessed.

"You hide it well."

"If they ever get us to their village—"

"They won't." Zach paused. "Your leg is worse, isn't it?"

"Don't worry about me."

"You can barely stand."

"I'll keep up."

"That's not what I asked."

"Shhhh."

"If I have to I can carry you."

Lou touched his cheek. "You wonderful idiot. How far do you reckon we'd get?"

"I'll have you climb on my back. We'll go slow. By morning we'll be down near the lake."

Suddenly a rabbit streaked by.

Zach shifted in the direction it came from, wondering what had spooked it. The answer was a who, not a what. He started to rise, but thought better of it. He would be dead before he took a step.

An arrow was centered on his chest.

Chapter Sixteen

Skin Shredder was beside himself. The war party had been his idea. He organized it. He led it. If it was successful, if he brought back captives, his people would hold him in high esteem. But he must return with all the warriors who went with him on the raid. Lose even one, and his people would say the raid was bad medicine. They would hold him to blame and whisper behind his back that he was a poor leader.

The Tun-kua had never been numerous. At their highest they numbered barely three hundred. That was before war with a much stronger tribe cost them many lives and forced them to leave the land they had called their own since they were formed from the clay of the earth. Now the Tun-kua numbered one hundred and sixty-seven. So many men had been lost in the war and on the long trek north that for every warrior there were three women. The loss of a single man was a cause for grief and dismay.

Bone Cracker was dying. His throat had been crushed by the half-breed, and he lay gasping and gurgling and convulsing.

"He was my friend," Star Dancer said sadly.

Skin Shredder glared at the captives and fingered his knife. Both were bound hand and foot and would stay that way until they reached the village.

"We should kill him here," Star Dancer said.

"You would deprive our people of his heart?" Skin Shredder snapped.

It would be worse than losing a warrior. He would be held in low regard by one and all. No one would ask his opinion in councils or want to go on a raid with him.

"No," Star Dancer reluctantly replied.

Bone Cracker arched his back. His mouth gaped wide and his tongue protruded, and with a final convulsion he gave up his spirit. A long exhale, and he was still.

Skin Shredder stepped over to the breed and kicked in the ribs him as hard as he could.

"Leave him be!" Lou cried. She had been dreading what the Heart Eaters would do.

Zach bore the punishment stoically. It would be a sign of weakness if he didn't, and he would be damned if he would give them the satisfaction.

"Here come Eye Gouger and Red Moon," Splashes Blood said.

The pair had gone after the two horses. They returned with only the black one. "We did not see the black-and-white horse," Eye Gouger reported, and wagged the bay's reins. "These were caught in a small tree or we would not have brought back this one."

Skin Shredder gnashed his teeth, a habit when he was angry. One warrior and one horse; he must not lose any more. He gestured at the captives.

"Throw these two over it." Maliciously, he made it a point to add, "Belly down."

Lou didn't resist when warriors took hold of her arms and legs. She guessed what they were about to do and tried to tuck at the waist to cushion the jolt, but they held her too tight. She was jarred to her spine, her stomach a riot of pain. Inadvertently she cried out.

Zach saw red. As the same two warriors bent to pick him up, he slammed his feet against the knee of one while simultaneously rearing up and butting the other in the groin. Both staggered back in pain. Rolling, he kicked the first warrior's other knee, eliciting a yelp, then swiveled to kick the other.

Skin Shredder couldn't credit his eyes. The breed was bound hand and foot yet he was about to bring down two formidable Tun-kua warriors. Uttering a screech of rage, he pounced. He drove his knees into the breed's chest, pinning him. Gouging his fingers into the breed's throat, he drew his knife.

"No!" Lou shouted.

Skin Shredder sneered at her. He pressed the tip to the breed's neck and a drop of blood bubbled.

"Please, no!" Lou knew he didn't understand the words, but her expression and the tremble in her voice were enough. She couldn't bear it if anything happened to Zach. She just couldn't.

Zach held still. Lou needed him. He must not provoke them any further—for now.

"Cut his nose off and force him to eat it," Star Dancer suggested.

Skin Shredder was about to, but he stayed his hand. Maybe it was the thought that his people would enjoy the ceremony more if they got to carve on the prisoner first. Lowering the knife, he barked, "Get him on the horse and we will be on our way."

Zach's ribs and chest were on fire. He submitted to being seized and was flung like a sack of flour up and over the bay, behind Lou. It didn't help his ribs any. His back was to Lou. He tried twisting so he could see her but a warrior poked him with an arrow.

Zach took the hint. They didn't want him talking to his wife. He waited until they were under way, then bent his head to whisper, "Are you all right?"

"Never better," Lou said, but she was scared, terribly scared. Not for her or for him but for the seed she hoped to nurture. She wasn't very far along, so the rough treatment shouldn't faze her, but it couldn't be good for her, either.

"I tried. I'm sorry."

"It's my fault we were caught again. I slowed you down. I'm the one who should be sorry." Lou had to stop. Emotion choked her at the thought that were they to die, she must shoulder the blame.

Zach would like to take her in his arms and comfort her. He settled for saying, "You're the best wife any man ever had."

"What made you say that?"

"It's true."

"You pick the darnedest times to be romantic."

Despite everything, Zach chuckled. He would be the first to admit he wasn't as tenderhearted as some men. His pa, for instance, was constantly bringing his ma flowers and giving her gifts.

Skin Shredder heard the half-breed chuckle and turned. It puzzled him greatly, this light-heartedness when they must know they were going to die. These Bear People, even those half and half, were truly strange. He didn't say anything. Let them whisper if they wanted. Before very long they would never whisper again.

The Outcast thought he was seeing things. The blow to the head had put his head in a whirl. But no, he blinked and the pinto was still there, nostrils wide and lathered with sweat. It had come trotting down the mountain and stopped when it saw him.

The Outcast went up to it. The pinto nuzzled his outstretched hand and rubbed against him. He stroked its neck, scratched behind its ears. "Where have you been? I thought I lost you in the rockslide."

His parfleche was still tied on. So was the club with the metal spike. Gripping the mane, the Outcast swung on and reined up the mountain.

The return of the pinto was an omen. All he needed was a bow and some arrows and he would be complete. The hideous warriors who took his captive had bows and arrows.

The Outcast thought of her eyes, the color of the lake. He thought of the times she had smiled. Most of all, he thought of her belly and what was in it, and he remembered Yellow Fox and what had come out of her.

He found himself thinking of Yellow Fox a lot. An irony, given that he had shut her from his mind for so long. What was it about the young white woman that caused this in him? He would be wise to slit her throat and be rid of her so she would not stir his memories.

The trail was easy to follow. The scarred warriors made no attempt to hide it. Evidently they felt they were safe. But they were wrong, as they would soon find out.

The Outcast untied the club with the metal spike. He tried a few practice swings. It had a nice balance, and the spike was sharp. He would rather have his bow, but the club would do. With it he could take out an eye, rip open a stomach, or pierce to the brain.

Overhead, the sun beamed. In the woods, birds sang. A butterfly fluttered by, making for the valley floor.

The Outcast climbed rapidly. The pinto was tired, but it had more than common stamina. He would let it rest later.

Time passed, and the Outcast came to a grassy bench. He rode up the slope to the top and drew rein in rare amazement at the sight before him. He scanned the forest and the slopes above, but there was no sign of anyone. For a while he stared at the body. Then he dismounted and squatted.

It was a scarred warrior, bare from the waist up. His arms had been folded across his chest. Someone had cut him from his sternum to his navel and pried the flesh apart.

The Outcast leaned closer. There was something missing, an organ. He realized what it was: the heart. Someone had reached in and cut out the heart.

This was new. This was different. This was bewildering. The Outcast knew of tribes that tortured and mutilated enemies. But he had never heard of any tribe, anywhere, that cut the heart out of one of their own. He tried to fathom why they had done such a thing. Then for them to ride off and leave the body for scavengers.

The Outcast rose and turned to the pinto. He would leave the body as it was. The strange thing they had done must be part of a ritual, and while he did not understand it, he did know it was not his place to judge how others reached out to the Great Mystery.

He was about to mount when he noticed a patch of color in the grass. A lump the size of his fist, most of it a reddish pink but parts slightly blue and purple. Puzzled, he walked over.

·It was the missing heart.

His bewilderment grew. Why cut out the heart only to throw it aside? He poked the heart with his club, then rolled it over. The other side was pockmarked with odd scoops taken out of it, half a dozen from top to bottom.

The Outcast went rigid with dawning horror. The marks were *bites*. Six of them—and there were six scarred warriors left. They had cut out the heart and each of them had taken a bite of it.

Gooseflesh prickled the Outcast. In all his winters, he had never heard of anything like this. He thought of the young woman who reminded him so much of Yellow Fox and of the heart beating in her chest. A chill rippled through him. It was a terrible way to die.

He climbed on the pinto and slapped his legs. A new urgency goaded him. He tried to tell himself that she had been nothing more than bait to lure her man to his death. He tried to tell himself that he didn't care about the new life in her womb. He tried to tell himself all this and more.

The Outcast firmed his grip on the club.

Soon.

Very soon.

Skin Shredder licked his lips. The taste of raw heart always whetted his hunger for more. Ever since his first bite when he had seen but six winters, he liked to eat heart more than he liked to eat anything. It was the same with all his people. The heart to them was more than meat. It was strength. It was power. When they ate the heart of another, they acquired some of that person's vital essence.

When one of their own died a violent death, they removed the heart and each of them took a bite. In doing so, they took into themselves part of the friend they were eating. It was the highest honor the Tun-kua gave their own. Many looked forward to having their hearts eaten. They dreaded dying of sickness because then their hearts would stay untouched and they would go into the next world without the mark of honor.

Skin Shredder would have liked to take Bone Cracker back to the village so that all his people could take part. But it would be several sleeps, and by then the body would bloat and give off an unpleasant odor, and the heart would not taste as sweet.

Skin Shredder glanced back at the bay. The white woman had a look of distress on her face, which pleased him. The breed showed no discomfort. He could bear much, that one, and would, too, before the Tun-kua were done with him. His mettle would be tested to its utmost.

The Tun-kua had tortured their enemies for as long as there had been Tun-kua. They didn't do it out of a desire to inflict pain. They didn't do it because they delighted in suffering. To them it was a test of courage, of manhood, of the warrior spirit. The more their enemy endured, the higher they regarded him. They ate his heart with the utmost reverence, for in the eating they took into themselves that which they most admired.

Skin Shredder couldn't wait to eat the breed's heart. He would cut it out himself. He had that right; the breed was his prisoner.

His shadow acquired a shadow of its own.

"I think we are being followed," Star Dancer said.

"You think?"

"I am not certain."

"What did you see?"

"What might be a man on a horse. But only for a moment. He is most careful not to be seen."

"One of the Bear People come to save these two?" Skin Shredder had been expecting it. He was surprised there wasn't more than one.

"I cannot say. He is too far off."

"Do we stop and wait in hiding?" Splashes Blood asked.

Skin Shredder pondered and came to a decision. "If we push on, we can be over the pass and in our valley by the rising of the sun."

Star Dancer said, "If I am right, the rider will follow us, perhaps all the way to our village. He will go to get other Bear People and they will come and try to wipe us out."

"He will not reach the pass. You will find a spot where he cannot see you and wait for him, and when he comes, kill him with arrows."

"It will be done."

Chapter Seventeen

Zach King wished he knew what the Heart Eaters were talking about. One of them had gone back down the mountain, and now the others were having an animated palaver. Zach got the impression that another warrior wanted to go with the one who left, but their leader was apparently against the idea.

Soon they resumed the climb. Zach twisted his head. Lou had turned slightly and was staring at him. She seemed pale and her lips were pinched tight, as they did when she was in pain. "How bad is it?"

"I have a cramp," Lou said. A bad one, above her hip. Her head hurt, too, no doubt from hanging upside down for so long. Her belly was sore, but not severely. So far she was holding up well, all things considered.

"I am thinking of trying to get away."

"Tied as you are?" Lou shook her head. "You wouldn't get twenty feet. It will make them mad."

"I have to try," Zach insisted. "I've been here before, elk hunting. The next slope isn't open like this one. It's covered with firs. I can lose myself, easy."

"How?" Lou was skeptical. "Burrow into the ground like a gopher? Climb a tree? Be sensible."

Zach fell silent. Even tied, he could hop, and if he picked the right spot, say a dense thicket or anywhere the brush was dense, he might elude them long enough to free his hands and feet. Then he could save Lou.

"Nothing more to say? You've giving up, just like that?" Lou's eyes narrowed. "I know better. I know you, Stalking Coyote, and you're still thinking of trying."

One thing Zach never did—or did as rarely as he could help—was lie to her. "I might not have a better chance."

"If you feel this strongly about it, we'll try together," Lou proposed. If she had to die, she preferred to die at his side.

"No."

"Why not? Haven't you heard?" Lou grinned. "What's good for the goose is good for the gander."

"It's too dangerous."

"Oh really? So it's all right for you to risk your life but not all right for me to risk mine?"

"You're risking two lives now. Or have you forgotten?"

"It's all I think of," Lou quietly admitted. Being told that women could have babies—being told that *she* could have one—didn't prepare a woman for the actual having. It was a miracle taking place in her own body.

The bay climbed higher, its reins in the hand of a stocky Heart Eater. Zach watched the warrior closely, noting how often he glanced back, which wasn't often at all. His bid to escape looked promising.

Lou was wrestling with herself. Zach was right. She shouldn't take chances. If he could get away she had no doubt he would rescue her.

Zach craned his neck, searching for the firs. They shouldn't be far off. He would drop from the bay and trust in Providence.

Lou saw him tense. "Please, Zach."

"Don't you dare beg me." It was the one thing Zach had no defense against. He couldn't refuse her anything when she begged.

"I just want you to be careful. For my sake and the sake of our child."

"Twice the reasons to stay alive," Zach joked, and regretted it when her features clouded.

Lou indulged in a rare cuss word. "You damn well better. I don't want to raise our child alone. If he takes after his father, he'll be a hellion."

Zach hadn't thought of that. If his son took after him—good Lord, the trouble he'd given his parents. He put it from his mind for the time being. Shadowed ranks of firs rose above, the trees so high and so close, they were in perpetual gloom.

Fear gnawed at Lou. Her head was telling her that Zach must try, but her heart was fit to burst with worry. She closed her eyes and swallowed, and when she opened them they were almost there.

None of the warriors was looking at Zach. He coiled his legs. Another minute, and they were in the trees, the Heart Eaters in single file, the bay in the middle.

Skin Shredder skirted a log and the rest followed suit.

Zach almost pushed off, but didn't. The warrior right behind the bay could see him. He waited.

A thicket was ahead. Skin Shredder motioned and headed around it, and was out of Zach's sight. Then the second and third warrior. The man behind the bay was looking at the ground, the last one at the sky.

It was now or never. Using his knees, Zach pushed and fell. A cushion of pine needles muffled the thud. As he hit, he rolled and then wriggled behind a fir.

The warrior behind the bay was still looking at the ground.

Zach grinned. When the last Heart Eater went by, he slid backward until it was safe to stand. Balancing on the balls of his feet, he began hopping. But it wasn't as easy as he'd hoped it would be. There were too many downed limbs and waist-high brush that tangled around his legs.

Zach thought of Louisa and the baby, and redoubled his effort. He must succeed for their sake. He would cut the ropes off and return to give the Heart Easters a taste of vengeance.

In midhop, Zach's left thigh exploded in pain. It felt as if an invisible hand pushed it out from under him, and he crashed onto his back. Fighting waves of agony, he looked at his thigh and discovered why.

The blood-smeared tip of an arrow jutted from his leg.

The Outcast stopped to rest the pinto twice. The slopes were steep, the day hot, and he had not come across water since morning.

The second time, he dismounted to stretch. Far below, the lake was a deep blue oval in a broad belt of green. Above, the lighter blue of the sky was sprinkled by high white clouds.

Wildlife was everywhere. He had spooked black-tailed does and bucks. Once, several elk trotted off at his approach. High on the crags, mountain sheep were occasionally visible. Twice he spied coyotes. Up here they were bigger than their lowland cousins; the ones he saw were almost as big as wolves.

Jays squawked at him. Red finches darted from tree to tree. Chickadees played in thickets. Juncos pecked the ground. He spied an eagle soaring with the clouds, the white of its head like snow.

The Outcast breathed deeply of the mountain air and reflected that of all the places he had been in his travels, he liked this valley best. It was a good place to live. The people in the wooden lodges had chosen well.

The Outcast ended his reverie and climbed back onto the pinto. He resumed his climb, the bay's tracks as plain as ever. Repeatedly, he glanced above him, and when next he did, he abruptly drew rein.

Something wasn't right.

All he saw were trees and brush and boulders. Nothing out of the ordinary about any of it—except he had the feeling that it wasn't. He scanned the pines and the shadows and saw no cause for alarm.

The Outcast had learned to trust his instincts. Often his life depended on them. He heeded his instinct now and stayed where he was. He searched and sorted what he was seeing in his mind for the slightest sign of danger. It all appeared as it should be.

After a while the Outcast tapped his heels. He rode at a walk, the club across his legs. Every patch of shadow merited scrutiny.

A cluster of blue spruce appeared. The trees' bark was dark, the limbs spaced close together. On an impulse he reined wide. He glanced away for an instant, distracted by a red-throated woodpecker that went flying past, and he heard a *twang*. Instantly, he threw himself from the pinto. The buzz of the shaft showed how near it came. He landed on his shoulder, rolled into a crouch, and was behind a boulder before another arrow could seek his life.

The pinto went a little way and stopped.

Placing an eye at the boulder's edge, the Outcast scoured the spruce. The archer was in there, somewhere, cleverly concealed. That there was just one surprised him. They were arrogant, these warriors with their scar tattoos.

The Outcast noted the lay of the terrain. He could not get close to the spruce without showing himself. They might be arrogant, but they weren't stupid.

Squatting, the Outcast mulled his options. He was at a disadvantage in that his weapons were for close combat. How to get close without taking an arrow? Rushing the spruce entailed too much risk. He could stay where he was and let the warrior come to him, but would the warrior be that foolhardy? Probably not. His other option was to wait for dark. Then he could slip into the spruce unseen. But by then the rest of the warriors might stop for the night and would be hungry. He remembered the heart and the bite marks and thought of the young woman, and her belly, and he resolved not to wait.

Scattered about were many small stones. Picking one, the Outcast threw it at the spruce trees. He did the same with a second and a third, throwing at random, hearing them strike and fall. Eight, nine, ten stones, and he picked up another and was about to throw it when an arrow streaked out of the air and missed the top of the boulder by a finger's width.

The Outcast ducked. He had seen where the arrow came from, high in the third spruce on the left. The warrior was well hid, but he was up a tree, which had a disadvantage of its own in that he could not move that quickly.

Flattening, the Outcast crawled toward a pocket of undergrowth. He was only in the open for a few moments, but it was enough. An arrow imbedded itself next to his arm. Then he was in cover and paused.

The Outcast put himself in the other warrior's moccasins. The man would begin to doubt the wisdom of staying in the spruce; he might decide to climb down.

Cautiously, the Outcast raised his head. A limb high up moved. Then the one under it. He had guessed right. He hurtled out of the brush, his legs pumping, weaving in case the warrior stopped descending to notch another shaft. He came to a spruce and dived behind it.

Nothing happened.

He figured the warrior was still descending

and hadn't noticed him. Pushing up, he started around the trunk and nearly ran into a shaft that thudded into the bark.

In the time it took the warrior to nock another one, the Outcast reached the next spruce. He put his back to the bole.

Now it was bobcat and grouse, and he was the bobcat.

His eyes darting everywhere, the Outcast worked around the trunk. He could see the tree the warrior was in, but he couldn't see the warrior. The man must be on the other side.

His moccasins soundless on the thick layer of pine needles, the Outcast circled, moving from tree to tree until he had an unobstructed view. The warrior wasn't there. He realized the man must have descended much faster than he thought.

They were both on the ground, and suddenly he was the grouse again.

The Outcast went prone. He had underestimated his enemy. An arrow could seek him at any moment from any direction.

The spruce were as still as death. The breeze had died. The birds had stopped singing. It was as if the forest were holding its breath, waiting for the outcome.

Quickly but quietly the Outcast moved to another tree. It had a wide trunk, and he felt safe in standing. Reaching up, he pulled himself onto a low limb. From there, he climbed to another. He peered around the right side of the tree and then the left. His enemy was nowhere to be seen.

It occurred to the Outcast that he was the one who had been arrogant. They were good, these scarred warriors. Their woodcraft was second to none, including his own. He went to climb down and froze.

A stone's throw away, beyond the stand of spruce, a vague shape crept through the undergrowth. It was the warrior, circling.

The Outcast slid behind the trunk. He was too easy a target. Dropping lightly to the ground, he dashed to another spruce. No sooner did he reach it than an arrow clipped his shoulder. The tip cut his buckskin shirt but not his own skin.

Crouching, the Outcast kept running. He raced out of the spruce and crouched in some brush, unscathed and wondering why. He had expected more arrows to fly. That none did suggested the warrior had used all the shafts in his quiver or had only a few left and wouldn't use another unless he was sure he wouldn't miss.

Staying low, the Outcast stalked toward the spot where he had last seen his enemy. Movement alerted him that the warrior was doing the same. He sank onto his stomach, the club at his side.

A cluster of dogwood moved.

But there was still no wind.

The Outcast gripped the hardwood handle with both hands. He coiled his legs, and when a dark form materialized low to the earth, he sprang. He vaulted high into the air with the club overhead. His adversary sensed him and looked up.

The club fell in an arc.

The warrior brought up his bow. Wood clacked on wood. The Outcast dodged a kick aimed at his knee. He avoided a thrust of the bow aimed at his eyes.

Snarling, the warrior heaved to his knees and grabbed for a long knife at his hip. The blade flashed, down low.

The Outcast sidestepped. He feinted to the left and stepped to the right and swung with all his might. Glinting in the sunlight, the metal spike buried itself in the warrior's eye. The spike was long enough and thick enough that it shattered the socket and penetrated to the brain.

The warrior pinwheeled his arms and kicked like a stricken frog, and went limp.

The Outcast wrenched the spike out. Gore and blood dripped from the metal. He shook it, then faced up the mountain.

There was more yet to do.

The Beginning

Night was about to fall.

Skin Shredder did not want to stop. His intent was to make it over the pass. But at a spring just above the tree line he called for a halt. Splashes Blood got a fire going while Eye Gouger and Red Moon went into the woods to gather enough firewood to last them the night. It was chill this high up once the sun went down, even in the summer. Head Splitter watched the horse and the captives.

His hands clasped behind his back, Skin Shredder paced. He didn't look up when someone began pacing beside him.

"You are worried about Star Dancer?" Splashes Blood asked.

"He should have rejoined us."

"I will take Red Moon and go look for him. If he has been slain we will avenge him."

"It would please me better if you stayed." Skin Shredder refused to risk losing more warriors. Two was bad enough; two was a calamity. His people would say he was bad medicine and shun him.

"He is our friend."

"One of the best we have," Skin Shredder conceded. "If he has been killed, I will want vengeance, too. But we have the two captives and the horse to think of. It is important we get them to our village."

Zach King saw their leader glare at him and wondered why. He had been dumped to the ground near the bay. His wrists and ankles were bound and his moccasins had been pulled off so if he ran, he would lacerate his feet to ribbons on the sharp rocks.

Lou stared at the dry blood on his thigh. "How are you holding up?"

"I keep telling you, I'm fine. They took the arrow out, didn't they?" Zach wasn't being completely honest. His leg hurt abominably, and he was burning with fever. The wound didn't appear to be infected, but he needed to clean and bandage it.

"They *yanked* the arrow out," Lou amended. It churned her stomach and made her queasy just thinking about it.

"Something is bothering them. The one who went down the mountain hasn't come back."

"Maybe it's Shakespeare," Lou said hopefully.

Skin Shredder walked over and kicked her. 'Be silent,' he signed. No matter how many times he told them, they kept on talking when his back was turned.

Zach surged up off the ground in anger, but he made it only as far his knees when Skin Shredder knocked him back down.

"I'm all right," Lou said. "Don't get them mad."

Skin Shredder turned to Head Splitter. "The next time either speaks, hit them with a rock."

"Hit to kill or to hurt?"

"We do not cut hearts from dead captives." Skin Shredder went to the fire. He was restless and irritable, and disliked being either. A warrior should have more self-control.

Splashes Blood held up a bundle of pemmican. "We found this in the breed's parfleche."

Skin Shredder took a piece. The others were already eating. "Give some to Head Splitter."

Grunting, Splashes Blood started to stand, and stopped. "Why is he standing that way?"

Head Splitter was leaning against the horse. His head lolled and his legs were wobbling. Suddenly the bay nickered and took a step, and Head Splitter oozed to the grass and lay on his side. The firelight played over the arrow that had transfixed him from back to front.

The Tun-kua sprang to their feet and moved toward him.

Exactly as the Outcast wanted them to do. By then he was behind them, the club in his hands. He could have killed more with the bow, but there were only four now—and he had seen their leader kick the young woman. He swung, and the metal spike buried itself in the nearest warrior's skull. The warrior stiffened but didn't cry out, and in a heartbeat the Outcast had tugged the spike out and was behind the next. This one he caught on the side of the head. The spike went in the ear and the warrior bleated and died.

The other two whirled.

The Outcast tried to jerk the spike out, but it was lodged fast in the bone. Letting go of the handle, he drew his knife and his tomahawk.

The two warriors drew their blades. The leader barked something and both attacked at once.

His arms a blur, the Outcast slashed, countered, stabbed. They pressed him hard. They were skilled, these two, but so was he. Blade rang on blade and knife rang on tomahawk. The leader cut his arm. The other sliced his side but not deep. He swept the tomahawk around and up and the keen edge sank into the other's throat, splitting the soft flesh and sending a scarlet spray every which way. That left the leader.

Skin Shredder saw Splashes Blood fall, and bounded back. He knew that alone he was no match for this warrior who had come out of nowhere and slain his friends with fierce ease, and as he saw no reason to needlessly throw his life away, he threw his knife, instead, at the warrior's face.

The Outcast ducked. The knife flew over his head, and he straightened to find the leader fleeing up the mountain with the agility and speed of a mountain sheep. He started to give chase but caught himself. To rush into the dark after an enemy who might be waiting for him was foolish. There would be another day. He turned toward the young woman.

"No!" Zach struggled to get between them.

The Outcast walked over to her. He avoided an attempt by the breed to kick him. He looked into her eyes and she looked into his. He saw no fear, not until she glanced at her husband, who was trying to reach him to kick at him again. The Outcast lowered his knife and cut the rope around her wrist and then the rope around her ankles. He sheathed his knife and reached down.

"Don't hurt her, damn you!" Zach shouted.

The Outcast thought she would recoil but she was unafraid. Pressing his hand to her stomach, he said softly, "Do you understand?"

Lou glanced down at herself. His words held no meaning but his gesture spoke volumes. She placed her hand over his and smiled.

The Outcast grew warm all over. His throat would not work. He coughed and stepped back. The breed had stopped trying to kick him and was staring at him in such astonishment, the Outcast laughed. "Take better care of her than I did of mine."

"What was that? I don't speak your tongue."

The Outcast smiled at the woman. He collected his club and the bow and quiver of arrows. He climbed on the pinto and rode to the south. The valley was big. At the south end was a mountain that interested him. Perhaps he would stay there a while. Perhaps he would stop wandering.

"What in the world?" Zach blurted.

"I think we have a new friend." Lou took a knife that had fallen to the grass, and freed him.

Zach was thinking of the one that got away. He dashed to the bay and took his pistol from the parfleche and made sure it was loaded. Then he swung up and extended his arm. "Climb on."

"But all these dead men and their weapons and whatnot?"

"I'll come back with Shakespeare. Right now I'm getting you home, where it's safe."

Louisa King tingled with happiness. "Home it is."

☐ **YES!**

Sign me up for the Leisure Western Book Club and send my FREE BOOKS! If I choose to stay in the club, I will pay only $14.00* each month, a savings of $9.96!

NAME: _____

ADDRESS: _____

TELEPHONE: _____

EMAIL: _____

☐ I want to pay by credit card.

☐ **VISA**　　☐ **MasterCard**　　☐ **DISCOVER**

ACCOUNT #: _____

EXPIRATION DATE: _____

SIGNATURE: _____

Mail this page along with $2.00 shipping and handling to:
Leisure Western Book Club
PO Box 6640
Wayne, PA 19087
Or fax (must include credit card information) to:
610-995-9274
You can also sign up online at **www.dorchesterpub.com**.
*Plus $2.00 for shipping. Offer open to residents of the U.S. and Canada only.
Canadian residents please call 1-800-481-9191 for pricing information.
If under 18, a parent or guardian must sign. Terms, prices and conditions subject to
change. Subscription subject to acceptance. Dorchester Publishing reserves the right
to reject any order or cancel any subscription.

DAVID ROBBINS

Doomsday. The end of all things.
Dreaded by many, scoffed at by skeptics.
And now it has come to pass.

At a remote site in Minnesota, filmmaker Kurt Carpenter has built a secure compound and invited a select group of people to bunker down until the worst is over. The world into which they reemerge is like nothing they've ever seen. At first they think they're the only ones left. But they soon find out how wrong they are. In the wasteland of what used to be America, their battle to survive is only just beginning...

ENDWORLD
DOOMSDAY

ISBN 13: 978-0-8439-6232-1

Paul Bagdon

Spur Award-Nominated Author of
Deserter and *Bronc Man*

Pound Taylor had been wandering the desert for days, his saddlebags stuffed with stolen money from an army paymaster's wagon, when he came upon Gila Bend. It was a wide-open town without law of any kind, haven to gunslingers, drifters and gamblers. Pound might just be the answer to a desperate circuit judge's prayers. He'll grant Pound a complete pardon on two conditions. All Pound has to do is become the lawman in Gila Bend. . . and stay alive for a year.

OUTLAW
LAWMAN

ISBN 13: 978-0-8439-6015-0

The Classic Film Collection

The Searchers by Alan LeMay

Hailed as one of the greatest American films, *The Searchers,* directed by John Ford and starring John Wayne, has had a direct influence on the works of Martin Scorsese, Steven Spielberg, and many others. Its gorgeous cinematic scope and deeply nuanced characters have proven timeless. And now available for the first time in decades is the powerful novel that inspired this iconic movie. (Coming February 2009!)

Destry Rides Again by Max Brand

Made in 1939, the Golden Year of Hollywood, *Destry Rides Again* helped launch Jimmy Stewart's career and made Marlene Dietrich an American icon. Now available for the first time in decades is the novel that inspired this much-loved movie. (Coming March 2009!)

The Man from Laramie by T. T. Flynn

In its original publication, *The Man from Laramie* had more than half a million copies in print. Shortly thereafter, it became one of the most recognized of the Anthony Mann/Jimmy Stewart collaborations, known for darker films with morally complex characters. Now the novel upon which this classic movie was based is once again available—for the first time in more than fifty years. (Coming April 2009!)

The Unforgiven by Alan LeMay

In this epic American novel, which served as the basis for the classic film directed by John Huston and starring Burt Lancaster and Audrey Hepburn, a family is torn apart when an old enemy starts a vicious rumor that sets the range aflame. Don't miss the powerful novel that inspired the film the *Motion Picture Herald* calls "an absorbing and compelling drama of epic proportions." (Coming May 2009!)

To order a book or to request a catalog call:
1-800-481-9191
Books are also available at your local bookstore, or you can check out our Web site **www.dorchesterpub.com**.

Author's Note

The accounts of the Tun-kua in the King journals have puzzled anthropologists and historians. Some say there was no such tribe. In Nate King's defense, a few observations are in order.

First, it is uncontested that before the coming of the white man, North America was home to hundreds of tribes. Exactly how many went extinct is uncertain, but the number is great. Some died of disease. Some were wiped out in war. Some assimilated into other tribes.

Migrations were another factor. Tribes drifted to better hunting grounds or fled from hostile tribes or moved to get away from the whites or were moved by force by the whites.

It is interesting to note that at one time there lived along the Texas coast a tribe called the Tonkahans. They were believed to be cannibals. No one knows what became of them. An account by an early Texas settler suggests they migrated "north."